THE
SHATTERED
VIOLIN

A Novel by

JARED BODNAR

For information, visit www.jaredbodnar.com.
Cover image by Josep Molina Secall
Cover design by Adam Garcia
ISBN: XXXXXXXXXXX
First Edition: July 2021
10 9 8 7 6 5 4 3 2 1

*To my mom, Gailee, who believed in me
when no one else would.*

CHAPTER 1

Cassie shoved the attacker away. She figured if she was able to get away from him, she hoped she could escape with superficial wounds.

The perpetrator was slicing her with an extremely tiny weapon. With a blade less than one half inch long, the pain was definitely being inflicted, but the cuts were not life-threatening.

She tried in vain to fight him off, blinded by the glint of the weapon reflecting off the table lamp. The attacker would pin her arms down against the baby-blue sheets with one hand and swing his other hand around and cut her body with the other. If she was able to squirm away with one hand, he would either push that arm down or pin it down deep into the mattress with a leg or his shoulders in order to continue to subdue her long enough to open her skin with the sharp object.

Cassie smelled faint laundry detergent as she fell off the bed. She saw some blood spatter on the mahogany floor. She then tried to roll underneath the bed, but the man grabbed her hair and slid her away from the bed across the wood floor. He continued to slice through her face and body with intention.

She grabbed her dark hair in her hand, trying to free herself and flee toward the front door. She caught a glimpse of the door, one that she'd walked through countless times, hoping that she hadn't just walked through it for the last time.

As much as she tried to loosen his grip, she found it futile and instead attempted to prevent him from cutting her further. She realized that the entire front of her body had been sliced and there were about fifteen to twenty lacerations on her face and neck area. Still, the wounds weren't deep, and although they would leave permanent scars, they were unlikely to cause her to bleed to death, or at least that was what Cassie was praying for.

She was unable to make out who her attacker was. But that didn't matter. All she wanted to do was get away from him. She was strong. She'd played scholarship soccer in college, which was very much a contact sport, resulting in more concussions than most Division I NCAA football programs. Cassie flipped over and dragged her feet under her, looking to use her legs to evade her attacker and get to the front door of her apartment.

It was no use. The tall and strong man was able to subdue her, using one hand to pin her to the ground and the other hand to complete methodical slices. Cassie was mostly silent, grunting as the potential killer maneuvered the weapon.

Instead of continuing, Cassie began to cry. "Help. Heeeeeelp."

She grabbed his hand again, trying to shield herself from the attack. It was useless. He was dominating her, and it was unlikely she would be able to free herself.

Even still, she was committed to resisting. She wasn't going to relent and let this person overpower her without a struggle. She was going to fight with all her might until the very end.

Her head slammed into the floor, and she looked at her pale arm as it rested in front of her eyes. Several drops of blood left her arm and rested on the floor in front of her. Not gushes of blood, but tiny drops of almost black blood, which contrasted with the dark brown wood.

Cassie again began to slither away, pushing her arms toward the attacker's face to mask the slices. He was undaunted by this and grabbed her throat, jamming the short, sharp item into her face and neck.

In defiance, she became obsessed with trying to wrestle the weapon away. She figured that if she could pry it from his fingers, she could stop the surface wounds from opening and perhaps even turn the tables on him to gouge his eyes or slice his neck, buying time for her to escape.

The more she tried to wrestle the small item out of his hand, the worse it became. He would just slam her head into the floor harder, or move the knife from her body to her face, defiling her attractive appearance. The blood droplets began multiplying, like burgundy raindrops pelting the silent planks of timber.

CHAPTER 2

Cassie's eyes fluttered open. It was a dream. A vivid and re-alistic dream, but a dream nonetheless. She surveyed her apartment to ground herself in reality.

Just then, a breeze whistled through the open window of her Seattle apartment, with the light from the sunrise entering like an uninvited guest. There was no other noise but the sound of her and her fiancé, Conner, lying in bed, shuffling under the covers. The sheets and down comforter were swirled around the couple randomly, meandering through their thin extremities.

Both on their backs gazing at each other, his bright grayish-blue eyes looked deeply into her hazel eyes. He continued to be surprised at how complex and beautiful her eyes were, even after staring into them for more than four years. They were impossibly intricate. The brownish rings that hugged her pupils faded into a yellowish color toward the edges of her irises. It was amazing to Conner how there was so much depth there, how much texture and how many flecks of color were present in those large, delicate spheres.

These impossibilities were complemented by long, curly, thick eyelashes—as if she was wearing mascara, although none was present. These familiar lashes provided the perfect frames for these gorgeous hazel rounds, in Conner's estimation. After contemplating the beauty of Cassie's eyes for several seconds, he blinked slowly and pursed his lips. Finally, he broke the silence.

"I love you so much," Conner let out of his pursed lips. His voice cracked on the word "much."

"I love you so much more," Cassie responded coyly, still trying to shake the impact of the vivid dream.

"You don't seem to understand," Conner uttered with all the seriousness of an FBI interrogator. "I love you more than you will ever know."

"You have no idea how much I love you, Conner," she responded casually. This one-upmanship could have gone on for hours and hours. This couple had always been known for being competitive, even between themselves. Although this particular exercise relied on no formal judging system based on quantitative measurements, Cassie and Conner were sure to be able to determine some sort of way to declare the winner of this rally.

Despite the fact that he was hell-bent on proving his enduring and incomparable love for her, Conner decided to surrender. "You know what?" Conner asked playfully.

"What?" Cassie quickly smiled.

"We are so disgusting." Conner giggled.

"Yeah." Cassie nodded while sucking in her cheeks. "Totally sickening."

Content with his peaceful end to the melee, Conner pulled his head away from hers and looked over at the window, watching the drapes move smoothly and randomly with the wind. She was a knockout to him, but she was also his perfect match emotionally. They achieved true intimacy, knowing everything about each other and accepting their deepest, darkest thoughts. Conner would often thank everything that was holy that she was his... that he had found the person who matched his wants and needs in so many ways.

As he looked out the window and saw the clouds rolling across the cornflower-blue sky, Conner thought about staring up at the clouds when they had traveled to Hawaii together. They found a secluded beach and stayed there for hours, staring at each other, holding hands, and talking about life and what seemed like the most earth-shattering topics at the time, but now seemed to be very mundane as he looked back at them.

He began to think about his deep feelings for Cassie. The calm and serene emotion that he got when he was with her. The way his heart still jumped a beat to this day whenever she got excited about something that she was passionate about. He looked at this as a kind of excitement empathy, but it was more than mere empathy. His heart raced with enthusiasm as if it was beating in the exact same rhythm as hers.

This morning reminded him of those precious hours sprawled out on the beach. The love he felt for her. All the great times they'd had together. All the struggles that they'd worked through together. The fights that always ended in spectacular make-up sex. He was perfectly content with her in every way, and he prayed that she felt the same way. He didn't want her to ever leave him and take away the one person who perfectly complemented him.

"What do you think?" Conner asked quickly. "Make a little love?"

"Oh, shit," Cassie said as she glanced at the unnecessarily large red digital numbers on the alarm clock that read 6:18. "I've gotta go. Sorry, babe." Cassie sprang up and hurled herself over the side of the bed, stumbling quickly toward the shower while almost losing her balance.

Conner let out a long sigh and put his hands behind his head, cradling his short sandy hair in between his long thin fingers. He stared up at the ceiling, thinking about the blow-out fight they had when they got back from Hawaii, sparring about money and the amount they spent on their vacation. Although they didn't always agree, they were always able to mend fences and come together in the end.

Conner felt the smooth wind that moved the translucent window coverings at random, the ridiculousness of his logical analysis of Cassie's internal and external features, and how the clouds careening through the azure sky couldn't hold a candle to the amazing person she was.

At five feet nine, she was taller and slenderer than any of her friends. Her skin was unusually light, like ivory. This contrasted with her almost jet-black hair, which she wore long and straight, down to nearly the small of her back. Her thin, athletic frame was envied by women and desired by men. Cassie's nose was round and curled up at the tip, accentuating her thick lips, which barely covered her well-proportioned piano key teeth, revealed whenever she exposed them from smiling or laughing.

He admired so many things about her. Her driven and ambitious nature, her lust for life, her sense of humor. She had a competitive streak like no one he'd ever meet. Not in a toxic, win-at-all-costs way, but in a way that inspired her to hustle, from being a scholarship soccer player in college to how she was highly motivated to win bar trivia contests. She wasn't perfect, though; Cassie had always been clumsy, oftentimes coming home with spilled-on clothes or broken shoes.

He knew full well he didn't have to get out of bed for at least another twenty minutes. She had to be at work by seven, and he didn't have to be at the junior high until seven thirty.

Again, he stared out the window at the blue sky and cumu-lus clouds, shaking his head, blasting a breath out of his nose, smirking at their inferiority.

CHAPTER 3

Cassie walked down Madison Street, clicking her heels on the pavement loudly as she clutched her stainless-steel commuter coffee mug in one hand and held her purse neatly in place with the other. This was a woman who exuded confidence. Not misguided bravado or arrogance, but true confidence born from being comfortable with herself and completely self-assured.

An overachiever since birth, Cassie had been goal-oriented and successful since she was quite young. Now a financial analyst for Getty & Lake, one of the largest accounting firms in the nation, Cassie had accomplished nearly every goal she'd set for herself, while also learning to deal with loss and defeat gracefully. Cassie was certainly not perfect. She'd made plenty of mistakes and missteps throughout her life, but she learned from them and made sure not to repeat them. And even with her substantial list of successes and much smaller list of failures, she still yearned for more, vowing not to be happy until she had achieved everything she set out to do—the list kept growing with each accomplishment.

The other source of confidence was surely her good looks. It was no wonder Conner was so taken with her physical appearance. Cassie had a unique mixture of classic beauty and modern appeal. Her soft facial features gave her a youthful image, but she also had a knowing and wise look, allowing her to effortlessly convey experience in a business environment.

Cassie casually glanced at her silver watch as she exited the elevator and made her way to her office, with its floor-to-ceiling window. If she leaned back in her chair and peered to the left of her desk, she could just barely see the Space Needle. Cassie was proud of her office, having worked in a cube for merely six months before being promoted, the shortest stint in a cube thus far in the company's history.

This had not come without hardship, however. Cassie struggled to find her groove in her first few years as a financial professional, having had a hard time transitioning from college to the business world. She was let go from her first company because of frequent mistakes and missteps. She found that she'd learned how to study and recite information in college, but not the practical skills needed to thrive in a business. After many struggles and hiring a mentor, she was gradually able to pull herself out of the tailspin and get better and better at her craft. This took several years, but she was able to turn it around, pay her dues, and relaunch her career.

Cassie slung her handbag over a chair and dropped into her seat, spinning toward her computer and stopping too far to the left, causing her to have to overcorrect the other way and grab her desk to get back in front of the keyboard to begin her sure-to-be-arduous day. She pecked away on her keyboard and called up her analytics report for the morning, stopping for a split second to rifle through her bag for a document, then immediately continuing to click away on her computer while intently following the numbers on the screen.

Without averting her eyes, Cassie lifted her coffee mug from the coaster where she'd placed it nearly two minutes earlier and took a small sip, warming her throat with the Italian roast. As she jerked the mug away, two teaspoons of the hot liquid splashed down on her shirt. "Oh, crud," she blurted as she looked down dejectedly.

Cassie's mind raced and heart pounded, thinking of how she could remedy this situation. She typically kept a few extra shirts around specifically for occurrences like this one. In this case, however, she was helpless. All of her backup shirts were at the cleaner's. Hurriedly, she trotted to the ladies' room and dabbed the fresh stain on her lapel with a wetted paper towel. This caused the stain to fade but still left a large round wet spot, which she prayed would go away by the time her first meeting started.

She strutted back to her desk, plopped down in her chair, and took a careful sip of coffee, hunching over while bulging her eyes out and looking down to make sure she didn't make the same mistake twice.

"Breakfast?" her colleague Dan yelled from just outside her office after poking his head in.

"Can't," Cassie responded without looking away from the screen. "I have a client meeting at nine sharp. I've gotta be on time." Who was she kidding? Cassie knew she would be there at least fifteen minutes early to make sure she was prepared for the meeting and everything was perfect. She was rarely late for a client meeting.

"Fine. Do you want anything?" Dan asked with a new, more casual tone. "I'm goin' down to Starbucks."

"I'm doing good," Cassie responded while raising her slim eyebrow and clutching her silver mug, shaking it gently into the air, silently cursing it for erupting on her minutes before. "Thanks, though."

Cassie had a feeling that Dan had a major crush on her, given multiple overtures over time. Conner also suspected that Dan had feelings for her based on her stories about him and other coworkers. Cassie put Conner completely at ease, and he had no cause to think there was anything going on between the two of them, or anyone else.

Dan left quickly, staring at the shiny floor as he walked away. Cassie finally looked away from her computer screen and shut the lid of her laptop. She grabbed the Lenovo computer, slapped some file folders on top of the thin laptop, and grabbed her cursed coffee mug, making her way quickly to the main conference room. As her heels tapped loudly and repeatedly on the slate floor, one of the female cube-dwellers looked up from what she was doing.

CHAPTER 4

Conner stood at the front of his classroom, just to the left of his beat-up desk. He was wearing an argyle sweater and pressed gray slacks with no pleats. Conner stood exactly six feet tall but only weighed in at 163 pounds. His skin had turned tan from playing flag football nearly every Saturday since the beginning of summer. This tan would surely fade now that school was back in session.

In addition to being tall, Conner was good-looking. His features were very well proportioned, with a roundish face, eyes set far apart, a long round nose, and a chiseled chin. In addition to his grayish-blue eyes and sandy blond hair, he had thin lips that Cassie frequently teased him about for no apparent reason.

Conner sauntered toward the whiteboard and picked up a dry-erase marker, scrawling "information sources" up on the board with little effort, as if he had written that phrase a million times before.

"Let's continue our discussion from yesterday. How do we know what is factual and what is not?" Conner asked his class of twenty-seven students, ages thirteen to fourteen.

"From a lot of different sources," said an ambitious Kelly Ferris from the third row of desks. "The news. Your parents."

"And how do we know the information they provide is factual?" he posited, grinning at another student in the third row.

"Research and experience," Kelly shot back immediately, not really knowing where her teacher was going with this line of questioning.

"And how do we know that's accurate information?" he asked in a more playful tone this time.

"Because someone who's been through something and has researched several different sources knows more than you do," Kelly said slowly, clearly annoyed by the restatement of the previous question.

Conner definitely had a point to his questions this morning. He had always taught his students to critically evaluate information and not just blindly accept information provided to them, no matter what the source.

"OK. Let's talk about information sources. I want everyone to write a source of factual information on the board and we are going to evaluate some of them," Conner said as he lifted his blue marker into the air.

Several groans emitted from the class as a few of the students begrudgingly arose and started heading toward the whiteboard. Others sat still, not wanting to be held up to ridicule for their answers.

Immediately, several words began to appear on the whiteboard in blue marker: "Newspapers," "Parents," "Textbooks," "Scientific Journals," "Teachers," "Friends," "The Bible," "The News," "Magazines," "Encyclopedias," "The Internet," "Facebook," "TV."

"Now I want everyone to go up to the board and put a number next to the information sources you think are most credible and least credible on a scale of one to ten. So, put a ten next to the source that you think is most credible and a one next to the source you think is least credible."

More slowly this time, students began to stroll up to the board and timidly mark their ratings of the information sources on the board. The students rose and made their way to the board as if they were outlaws heading toward the gallows in their final moments. They knew full well that Mr. Denton would arbitrarily select students to share their answers if none picked up markers voluntarily.

The traditional information sources received high marks, particularly the news and encyclopedias. The largest swing in ratings were between friends, parents, and the Bible, which were rated as high as ten and as low as zero, which Conner realized was outside of the rating scale but ignored anyway.

Conner had a feeling his students knew where he was going with this exercise. It was interesting to him how different people judged information sources in numerous ways, or not at all. But his entire goal was to instill some sort of semi-objective evaluation system his students could use to determine which information sources to trust.

"All righty," Conner said whimsically. "Why was the news rated so high by so many people?"

"Because," Robert coughed with his raspy voice. "They are responsible for reporting only the facts, and people would call them out on it if they lied."

"That's not true," said Kelly Ferris again. "They are responsible to the corporations that own them, so they are biased based on what their CEOs want you to hear."

Conner squinted his eyes at Kelly, recognizing her as a critical thinker in the making. "Where do these news sources get their facts from, these so-called corporations that own them?"

"They get them from a variety of sources. Witnesses to the news. The AP. Other news agencies," piped up Matthew from the back row.

"OK, so how do we know all those sources are credible?" Conner asked, now a little frustrated with himself that he'd repeated essentially the same question several times.

"We don't. That's the point," insisted Kelly. "Since they get their information from a variety of places, you can't really be sure they're telling the truth. You have to research the information yourself."

"And how do you research that information?" Conner shot back instantly. "What information sources do you use?"

"It depends on what type of information you're looking for," Kelly said, realizing she was dominating the discussion. "If it's scientific information, you would consult scientific journals; if it's information about a crime or fire, you'd have to go to the police or fire department."

"Well, isn't that a bit cumbersome?" Conner asked skeptically. "Why not just take the news organization's word for it?"

"Because," Kelly said. "You'll never know if someone is being truthful unless you investigate it for yourself."

"But how do you investigate it for yourself?" Conner questioned. "What standards would you use to evaluate the information you found in the scientific journals, for example? Would you just take that at face value?"

Kelly sat there thinking. The rest of the class just sat quietly, recognizing that the group discussion had turned into a two-way conversation. Acknowledging this himself, Conner asked another follow-up question to the group.

"How many of you ranked your parents as a ten?" Conner asked as he raised his own hand.

After noticing a half dozen hands shooting into the air, he singled out Robert. "Robert, why do you think your parents are such a credible information source?"

"I think your parents want to give you good information because they want you to have the facts when making decisions," Robert mumbled.

A voice shot right back at him, one that was not in the original group of parent-trusting hand raisers, but thankfully not Kelly's, who at this point realized she should take it easy and let others speak.

"But don't you think your parents tell you lies in order to protect you?" said Maxine. "Don't they sometimes tell you what they want you to hear rather than the truth, just to get you off their back?"

"I don't think so," Robert whimpered. "I think my parents want what's best for me, and they're willing to tell me the truth even if it could hurt me in the end."

"They do say the truth hurts," Conner expressed, hoping to get a few laughs but settling for two subdued chuckles.

"What other information sources did we rank as very credible?" Conner continued.

"The Bible," shouted Clarence from halfway back in the middle row of desks.

"And why is this such a credible source of information?" said Conner after clenching his teeth, knowing full well that he worked in a public school and any religious discussion could get him into hot water.

"Because it's the inspired word of God," Clarence said with a self-satisfied tone that almost made Conner think the next word out of his mouth would be "duh."

"What about the internet?" said Conner, quickly distracting his students from having a theological discussion in a public-school classroom. "Why did so many of you rank that so low?"

"Because anyone could post anything on the internet, whether it's true or not," said Kelly, modestly exerting control over the discussion once again.

"I noticed a lot of you ranked encyclopedias as high on the list. What about Wikipedia?" Conner asked as a follow-up.

"It's the same thing as the internet," Kelly said. "Anyone can contribute to Wikipedia, so it's not a very credible source of information."

"But don't you have to cite your sources on Wikipedia? That makes it more credible," said Matthew from the back of the room.

"Not really," said Kelly. "The sources that they use may be wrong as well. It's like..." Kelly desperately searched for the right words as she looked to the ceiling of the classroom. "It's like saying the facts are what everyone agrees on rather than using... science."

"Ah, science," Conner interrupted. "Let's talk a little more about science."

As the classroom began to further continue their discussion, a light rain began falling outside. Whenever it rained, the classroom began to smell musty from an old bookshelf that was positioned next to the window, crammed with dusty books about methodological reasoning and English humanities.

Conner just imagined himself eating a nice dinner at the end of the day.

CHAPTER 5

As Conner opened the door to the apartment, he shut his eyes tightly and blinked a few times. After taking a deep breath while shutting the door behind him, he sighed to himself. "I'm fried."

It was a taxing day for him. One of Conner's idealistic goals in teaching the next generation of leaders was moving away from standard lectures and rote memorization and challenging his students to think independently, to see the big picture, to critically analyze information using the scientific method. By engaging his students in a spirited discussion rather than giving them reading assignments and lecturing to them day in and day out, he had to work twice as hard as other teachers in his school, and thus he tended to become exhausted and beat by the end of the day.

Conner collapsed into the couch and took a nap. About two hours later, he was awoken by the faucet turning on and off quickly. Cassie was making dinner. He smelled basil and roasted red pepper. He heard vigorous chopping.

Among the many things Conner loved about Cassie was her cooking. Without any sort of formalized training or recipes, Cassie managed to whip up restaurant-quality fine dining on a nightly basis. This was clearly a function of her growing up in a family that revolved around food. Cassie learned the tricks of the trade from her mother, who adored food and planned every family event around bountiful meals. The family was always engineering neighborhood barbecues, family picnics, church potlucks, and dinner parties. She surely picked up her improvisational skills from her mom, who always cooked without a recipe.

Without looking up from her cutting board, Cassie cleared her throat and asked Conner an obvious question. "How was your day, dear?"

"Exhausting." Conner sighed. "Whatcha makin' tonight?" he asked in a singsongy way, with all the rhythm of a Norwegian yodeler.

"Chicken cutlets with a pesto sauce, and polenta casserole," Cassie answered back seductively. Conner felt a chill go through his entire body, starting from the tip of his skull all the way down to the small of his back. Cassie knew that Conner found it damn sexy whenever she talked about food. As he resisted the urge to throw her down on the kitchen tile and have his way with her right then and there, he swallowed the lump that had quickly accumulated in his throat and thought better of it.

"Sounds super yummy," Conner sang, one octave down this time, playing with the pile of mail on the charcoal granite countertop. "How was your day, babe?"

"Actually, it went unbelievably well," Cassie said in an unusually upbeat tone. "My client meeting was phenomenal, and I was just in a rhythm. Things are going really great for me at work."

"That's awesome, baby," he said while trying to sound like he wasn't insincere, even though he was in fact being genuinely sincere. "I'm proud of you."

Conner always knew Cassie would be the breadwinner in the family, and he had no problem with that. He chose to pursue his passion for teaching, knowing full well she would always make at least twice as much money as he did. While some of his friends seemed to have a problem with this inequality, and some people viewed this as emasculating, Conner was completely confident with his situation. He even mentioned to some of his friends on occasion that all the pressure was on her, so he could do whatever he wanted with his life. With money not being a factor, he was free to chase his dreams.

Conner looked at Cassie with loving intensity as she went about her perfectly conducted orchestra in the kitchen. He couldn't believe she was actually his. He loved her so deeply and he couldn't imagine life without her. Everything about her was attractive to him. Everything was poetic perfection.

Conner began to reflect on the first meal she ever cooked for him. They had just started dating and she cooked him meatloaf, one of the meals he said he loved as a kid. This gourmet meatloaf was the most wonderful concoction he had ever tasted, and he began to fall in love with her at that moment. Not only because they were having an amazing conversation, not only because she was a wonderful cook, not only because she was stunning, and not only because she had an amazing sense of humor and she laughed at most of his obscure jokes.

He began to fall in love with her that evening because she was so thoughtful. As a result of a comment he made in passing about the meatloaf his mom used to make him growing up, Cassie decided to whip up this culinary delight. She listened to every word he said and made mental notes about what he liked and disliked, planning this meal just for him.

This was certainly not the last thoughtful thing Cassie did to make Conner happy. In fact, they both strived to be very thoughtful and do kind things for each other. Like the time Conner bought Cassie a Slap Chop after she mentioned how cool it was after seeing it on an old infomercial.

"The guy hocking that thing is a total sleaze, but how cool would it be to have one of those things?" she asked Conner that night as her head rested on her lap while they were watching TV on the couch. Sure enough, the Slap Chop materialized a week later and she appreciated the kind gesture, making fun of the smarmy pitch man as she tried it out for the first time. "Check out these nuts," she said with a slap of her wrist.

After daydreaming about those memorable moments in their life together, Conner averted his gaze, being careful not to stare at her for too long for fear that he would be like Perseus glancing at Medusa and turn to stone by admiring her allure for an extended period of time. He decided to start setting the table for the meal that was sure to be wonderful.

As they dined on her delicious meal that night, Conner peered into Cassie's impossibly attractive eyes. They chatted about what was going on in the world at the moment, the precocious student who was dominating the discussion in Conner's classroom that day, the great feedback Cassie's client gave her on her meeting, a trip the two had planned to Costa Rica. Their future together. The simple things that made their life together simply wonderful.

CHAPTER 6

Twip. Thwip. Thwip. The sound resonated through the small storefront warehouse, and Conner's brother, Joseph, ran a card scraper over the top of a baby grand piano. The smell of fresh wood shavings filled Conner's nostrils.

He began to think about the wood that unwillingly sacrificed itself to create this particular piano. Where did it come from? Was it wood from one of the nearby old-growth forests in the state of Washington, or was it from Italy, China, or South America. How long ago was the tree chopped down? At what point was it destined to become a piano? Was it maple, elm, birch, or some other type? Had two young lovers ever scarred the tree's flesh by scratching their initials into the bark to communicate to future generations that they were truly in love.

Conner began to admire his brother's handiwork. Joseph was gifted in all types of musical instrument restoration. While some piano refinishers and musical instrument repair shops specialized in just one or a select few types of instruments, Joseph fixed and renovated them all. Acoustic and electric guitars, violins, pianos, cellos, woodwinds, saxophones, trumpets, drums—everything.

He also put his everything into his craft, sacrificing countless nights and weekends repairing instruments that had been damaged or worn down from years of use. His brother had built a nice business for himself through word of mouth. Most every professional musician who had ever needed an instrument repaired or restored in the Seattle area knew the name Joseph Christopher Denton.

"So what are you doing this weekend?" Joseph asked his older brother, not looking up from his work.

Conner replied, somewhat uninterested, focused more on the precision of his brother's hands as they slid the tool across the flecked wood of the piano. "Dunno. May go to the Seahawks game. Otherwise, we'll probably just hang around the apartment. What about you?"

Conner knew what Joseph was going to say before he said it.

"Going kayaking up at Puget Sound," Joseph said with excitement in his voice. Conner rolled his eyes a bit, knowing almost instinctively that this was his brother's favorite pastime.

Joseph had always been an outdoorsy type, unlike Conner. He loved to go hiking, camping, kayaking, rock climbing—anything having to do with the outdoors.

In addition to enjoying outdoor activities, Joseph was something of a hippy, wearing his blond hair long and currently wearing a flowing button-down shirt with no collar, which consisted of some natural material unknown to Conner. Probably hemp or flax or something weird like that. Joseph looked a bit like Conner but with a bigger nose and lighter blue eyes, almost white, like smoked glass with a milky bluish coating. He was also a good five inches taller than Conner and had a dusting of freckles that dotted his larger schnoz. Conner had maybe two freckles on his whole body, so he wasn't sure where his sibling inherited that recessive genetic trait.

"Sounds fun, dude. Say hi to Mother Nature for me," Conner joked.

Conner always enjoyed spending Thursday evenings at his brother's shop. They would go to a local organic coffee shop and grab a few lattes and then sit in the warehouse and chat while Joseph restored the instrument du jour.

Conner liked the pungent smell of linseed oil that permeated his brother's shop, contrasting with their espresso-based drinks. He was very proud of his brother. Music had always been Joseph's passion, and he got into the instrument restoration business after he cracked the neck of his bass guitar in half after a gig with his jam band. Joseph researched woodworking and musical instrument repair in detail, opting to fix his precious instrument himself rather than entrusting another person with it. After success and newfound passion, he began to fix other people's instruments and restore antique instruments, working as an apprentice at first and then opening up his own business when the demand, and his skills, warranted it. Conner could tell that his brother loved what he did, and he appreciated the fact they were both able to follow their dreams, not work for a gigantic corporation that treats you like a number, as he'd seen Cassie and others treated on numerous occasions.

Although Conner wouldn't consider himself a hippy like he considered his brother Joseph, they shared a lot of similar views about society and politics. Of course, they disagreed on many things as well, but they were always able to argue constructively, not taking any of their political differences personally.

They both shared a deep distrust for the government and had a problem with rules and laws they viewed as arbitrary.

Conner frequently joked that he had a hard time following the rules, whether it be traffic laws, guidelines about how he was supposed to teach his students, or even some of the innocuous rules of the flag football league he played in.

The brothers would get into passionate discussions about the original intentions of the Founding Fathers of the United States, the Federalist Papers, and how their best-laid plans had been dashed by the greedy politicians and political system of today, which they both looked at as rife with corruption and driven by the almighty dollar.

This night in particular was one of quiet reflection and surface banter—what they were going to do on the weekend, who was going to win the Seahawks game, how Cassie was kicking ass and taking names at work, nothing too deep. Nevertheless, despite the topic of conversation, Conner and Joseph always enjoyed their time together.

CHAPTER 7

Cassie strolled down Mercer Street, clutching her purse and talking on her iPhone. A sea of people poured down the street surrounding her.

"I can't make it," she insisted. "I just can't." On the other end was her colleague Doug, who was asking her to fly to New York City the next week for a new business meeting.

"This would be a huge client for us, Cassie," Doug stressed with the disciplined intensity of a lawyer giving his closing argument.

"My client is only going to be in town until the seventeenth, and I really need to cover a lot with them. So I apologize, but I just can't do it this time," Cassie said.

Cassie was frequently asked to participate in new business pitches, even though her schedule was rather hectic. Cassie always felt as though she was being pulled in several different directions and not able to dedicate her time to one specific task at a time. Although she was flattered people requested her involvement in such important meetings and activities, she didn't feel it was fair to her current clients for her to be spread so thin. In most cases she would say yes, but she couldn't this time. Her very best client, in terms of dollars and meaningful work, was in town just until Wednesday of next week, making a trip to New York on Monday impossible.

Cassie thought back to her college days, learning about accounting and finance and not thinking she would ever venture into sales. And while her passion was clearly in solving problems and surfacing insights with financial models, she found joy in bringing new clients in. As a competitive person, she was exhilarated when pitching potential clients and closing big deals. Doug knew this charged her up, so he pressed on.

After continuing to hold her ground, Doug gave up. "All right, I'll see if Jenna can go."

"I'm really very sorry, Doug. I..." Cassie was distracted by an abstract shape she saw out of the corner of her eye. She glanced over at a male figure draped in a dark blue raincoat across the street.

He was a very tall man, with an imposing presence. She quickly noticed his hands were clenched into tight fists, his blue boots were slightly darker than his raincoat, and he appeared to be shifting from one foot to the other. She couldn't make out his face, as it was obscured by the raincoat hood, but he was glaring at her... motionless. Rain pelted his head, shoulders, and face. His figure looked strangely familiar.

Cassie extended her head to try to ascertain whether who she was looking at was who she thought he was. After a couple of seconds of staring in his direction, the person's face turned away, almost looking like a speed skater as he cut through the crowd and the rain. A gray Amazon Prime delivery truck passed between them as she turned in the other direction.

"I gotta go," Cassie nervously said. "I apologize again. Goodbye."

Cassie tapped on the screen and nervously shoved the phone into her purse. "Taxi," she screamed at the top of her lungs with her hand outstretched. After watching two taxi-cabs pass by her with passengers inside them, which felt like an eternity, a faded yellow cab screeched to a stop twenty feet ahead of her. She scurried over to the cab, trying not to slip in a river of rain that flowed through the street. Waiting until the door slammed shut, she directed the driver, "Union and 18th Avenue, please."

The taxi sped away as Cassie looked behind her, seeing no one.

CHAPTER 8

The door of their apartment shut with a loud clink behind him. Conner clenched his eyes shut, then slowly opened them again. Another arduous day in the classroom. This time, he'd instructed his students to compare studies that were circulating in the media regarding teenage pregnancy. He asked his students to evaluate two articles, one claiming abstinence-only education decreased teenage pregnancy and the other claiming that sex education including birth control information lessened the incidence of teenage pregnancy.

"Babe," Conner said with a large exhale. "Where are you?" He heard no chopping. Smelled no basil. Heard nothing.

Conner raised one of his eyebrows then closed his eyes tightly once again and walked toward the kitchen. As he turned the corner, he saw Cassie leaning up against the kitchen island, her arms crossed on the dark granite, cradling her chin with her thin fingers. Seeing her chew her lip thoughtfully, it was obvious she was pondering something.

What's up? Conner thought. As he started to slowly open his mouth to ask this question, she answered.

"I swear, I think I saw him today."

An icy chill raced through Conner's entire body. He knew exactly who "him" was: Cassie's ex-boyfriend from college. The one she broke up with her last semester before graduation. The one who stalked her for three months. The one who called her and hung up repeatedly every single night for months. The one who drove by her dorm every day and sat outside her building in his car. The one who threatened her life on several occasions. The one who drunkenly threatened her with an X-Acto knife at a house party. The one she never wanted to see again. The one who may have just walked back into their lives. The name Conner would never forget. Seth Warner.

Conner thought for a split second about the chosen weapon Seth wielded, in a belligerent state, at that fateful party. Thankfully, several people tackled him to the ground and wrestled the unconventional weapon away.

"Are you sure?" Conner asked. He did not want to utter Seth's name and reopen the emotional wounds that this clearly disturbed man had inflicted on the love of his life.

"No," Cassie choked out. "I'm not sure, but I think it was him. I saw someone who looked like him for a split second, and then I jumped right into a cab and left." She was obviously getting worked up and started breathing heavily.

"What should we do?" Conner asked with urgency. "Should we call the police?"

"No," Cassie insisted. "They can't do anything anyway. I'm not even sure it was him, and he hasn't contacted me or threatened me."

The only time the police were ever involved was the night of the house party. The campus police came and broke up the disturbance. Cassie decided not to press charges. She never called the police. She never reported him for harassing or stalking her. She never filed an order of protection against him. Nothing. When explaining the situation to Conner,

Cassie expressed that she was biding her time before graduation. She figured all she had to do was make it to June, graduate, and move away. She'd never see him again. She made sure she left no trace when she moved, first to the Bay Area and then to Seattle. There was no sign he'd found her, until today, more than ten years later.

"We have to do something, Cassie," Conner insisted. "You could be in danger."

"I'm not even sure it was him," Cassie shrugged. "If it was, I'm not sure what to do."

"I say we go to the police," Conner urged. "We can get a restraining order against him and see if they can keep tabs on him or something."

Just as those words came pouring out of Conner's mouth, he realized how ridiculous they sounded. They had no reason to get a restraining order against him. They couldn't prove anything. There was virtually no documentation that demonstrated this pattern of behavior. They didn't even know if it was him or, if it *was* him, what his intentions were. Maybe he'd sought help for his obsession issues and turned his life around, acknowledging the error of his ways. Conner said a little prayer to himself, squeezing his eyelids shut once again. He hoped that these were the reasons for Seth's reappearance in her life, if it was him.

Conner and Cassie ordered Chinese takeout that night, talking at length about the situation. They jointly decided to be cautious and aware. They needed to first determine if it was, in fact, Seth. Then they could take appropriate action.

CHAPTER 9

Weeks went by. There was no sign of the figure in the blue raincoat. Cassie went about her daily routine, cautiously looking out for another glimpse of her obsessed ex-boyfriend. Conner did the same thing when they were together, using descriptions of Seth's appearance relayed by her. Still, nothing. Not a glimpse. The couple began to think the person she'd spotted was just a similar-looking person and not the person they feared he was. Maybe it was just a figment of her imagination brought back from the trauma he caused.

Conner pressed on at work, trying desperately to turn his students into critical thinkers. He was making a tremendous amount of progress with Kelly Ferris. She was, by her nature, inquisitive and curious. She was the perfect raw material he could use to influence his entire class and transform them into thinkers, rather than passive consumers of information. He found that once he began to get through to one student, they could positively infect the entire class with the critical-thinking bug. He hoped against hope that he was making progress.

Cassie was progressing quite well at her firm. She was getting better and better at multitasking every day. She found a clever way to juggle her demanding clients with her new business efforts. The top executives at her firm certainly recognized her impressive closing rate. Three out of five prospective clients signed on with the firm when Cassie was involved with the pitch, as opposed to the standard closing rate of 20 percent. She was well on her way to advance to expanded roles within the company.

From the beginning of their relationship, they had always been adventurous and unconventional. They would opt to take weekend road trips and flights out to the San Francisco Bay Area, Las Vegas, Phoenix, New York. But Cassie would be creative with her getaways, once even meeting Conner at his school at the end of the day with tickets to the Mariners game tucked into her Daisy Dukes, with a loose-fitting Mariners jersey tied at the front—suitcase at her side to see them play out of town.

Conner thought she was the sexiest thing alive, even when she was wearing baseball gear or lounging around in sweats and a tank top. He admired the fact that she could pull anything off. She had such a versatile style that made her equally attractive whether she was in her corporate power suit, a jet-black evening gown, or the overalls she wore when they repainted their apartment.

When Cassie started to dig through Conner's drawers to find something to wear, he was immediately turned on. His shirts were way too big on her and she had to double-fold his boxer shorts so they'd fit her slender frame. Conner would look longingly at her as she strutted around the bedroom in his clothes. He gave her a few minutes to get comfortable in the bed before he joined her and removed the shirt and boxer shorts, kissing her passionately while his fingers found their way around her body.

CHAPTER 10

Conner's head fell heavy into the pillow, rolling off of his lover, out of breath and filled with adrenaline after intense sex. As he lay there next to her, sweat beaded on his forehead and streamed down onto the pillow. Conner appreciated their sex life. From the first night they had sex, Conner knew there was something special about their connection in the bedroom. It was almost as if their two figures were cast together in plaster to create a sculpture, broken in two after they hardened, and then pieced back together every time their bodies connected in ecstasy.

They loved sex together. They both enjoyed experimentation, role-play, sex in public, toys, impact play, and bondage. He could bring her to orgasm within seconds, her entire body shaking. Feeling her give in to the moment overwhelmed him with excitement and passion.

Intense orgasms were not only enjoyed by Cassie. Conner had mind-blowing, earth-shaking, scream-inducing orgasms with Cassie. Something that he had never experienced with previous lovers.

They were both very vocal in bed. After being in a long-distance relationship for several months and having to rely on phone sex, they had brought this dirty talk with them into the bedroom. Conner reinforced the fact that everything she uttered or groaned in bed was a major turn-on for him.

In one of their first sexual experiences together, Cassie uncontrollably yelled out the phrase, "This is perfect." Conner shot her a look of confusion. Then recognized he couldn't have put it better himself. They were sexual soul mates, perfectly matched in every way—physically, emotionally, intellectually, and spiritually.

"God, I love you so much, baby," Conner exhaled, still weak.

"I, I love you... too, Conner," whispered Cassie, still shaking and experiencing aftershocks from her orgasms. "You make me feel so, so, so... good, Conner."

He loved when she said his name, especially during sex. It made him feel good about himself. A confident, self-assured man. He loved nothing more in life than pleasing her sexually and emotionally. As he rolled his head over to the edge of the pillow, he began his ritual of gazing into her eyes, pursing his lips, and squinting his eyes at her beauty. As he admired her, he reminded himself once again of how outrageously lucky he was to find this woman. This woman who loved him in every possible way.

CHAPTER 11

"Let's have a picnic," Cassie enthusiastically yelped as she shut the lid on her trusty Lenovo laptop. Conner glanced over from his crossword puzzle and raised both eyebrows. "OK. Let's do it," he exclaimed. Conner knew better than to refuse such an offer. When Cassie was able to stop working before noon on a Saturday, it was a momentous occasion, and one he wouldn't dream of passing up for a second.

Conner and Cassie raced into the kitchen and began to gather items together for their picnic. Cassie hummed an unfamiliar song, grabbing several items out of the refrigerator. She began to assemble them into edible goodies they could take to the park with them. Conner knew full well what his role was—to grab the wine, silverware, and plates.

The couple neatly packed all of their items and set off for Kerry Park. They walked several blocks and found a spot on the green grass, where they usually picnicked while gazing at Elliott Bay. They laid down a blanket and toppled down perpendicular to each other. Conner rested his head on Cassie's slender belly. "I can hear your tummy growling," he sang to Cassie.

"I know. I'm hungry, but I'm too tired to eat." Cassie laughed back. The couple drifted off to sleep under a large tree. With birds chirping and the smell of freshly cut grass wafting in and out of their nostrils, the couple found themselves in full relaxation mode.

When they regained consciousness, it was almost sundown. They were in different positions now, so Conner arose and shook her elbow. "Wake up, babe. You're missing your own picnic," he joked.

But Cassie wouldn't awaken.

"Babe?" Conner nudged. "Wakey wakey," he said playfully.

"Hhhhmmff," Cassie grunted. "I'm up," she said as she drearily arose with her eyes still closed and made her way toward the picnic basket.

They sat and watched the sunset, eating finger sandwiches, cheese, and pita chips.

"People don't really go on picnics anymore, but it's such a fun thing to do," observed Cassie.

"Great point. I don't see one other picnic in the vicinity," Conner agreed. "In fact, why don't we start a picnicking movement, perhaps starting the uprising on Facebook."

"We could be single-handedly responsible for a resurgence of picnicking in the United States," Cassie said as she grinned.

"What's in it for us?" Conner posited. "We'll just create more crowds and gridlock in the parks we know and love. It wouldn't make any sense unless we get into the picnic-basket-selling business."

As the birds chirped, the young lovers laughed at each other... and at themselves.

CHAPTER 12

Conner rarely worked late. Sometimes he would hold office hours to meet with his students on a one-on-one basis, or help with an after-school program, but usually he would immediately head home. But tonight Conner was appealing to his school superintendent for more funding for scientific endeavors. Conner gave a spirited presentation on this topic, citing research that showed students who were involved with science- and math-based curricula performed better on standardized tests and had a higher college acceptance rate. He was sure that Marla, the superintendent, would respond to the increase in standardized test scores. The district was obsessed with improving standardized test scores. He definitely knew his audience.

After the presentation, Conner headed home. Marla said the school board would review his proposal and provide him with an answer in the coming weeks. As Conner walked up the steps, he looked forward to talking to Cassie about the presentation. He wondered what questions she'd ask, and he started formulating his responses.

Conner stepped out of the elevator and ambled toward the door of the apartment, making loud clacking sounds on the tile as if he was wearing tap dancing shoes. He ran his fingers through his hair a couple of times and rubbed his eyes gently with his thumb and forefinger. It was good to be home.

The door was slightly ajar when he got to the apartment. Conner was perplexed and, for a split second, concerned. Cassie never left the door open. Maybe she'd just run out to get the mail and hadn't bothered to shut the door, prancing down the hall to retrieve their stack of bills and periodicals. Then, maybe something was wrong. He felt the pit of his stomach drop. What if there was an intruder? Wait. What if it was Seth Warner? Had he tracked her down and attacked her? Not wanting to think negative thoughts, he placed his hand gently on the door and pushed it open cautiously.

The first thing he saw was two uniformed police officers shooting him concerned looks. *Oh*, he thought, *maybe the alarm went off and...* Conner looked closer, inspecting the apartment. As he looked past them, Conner could see a large crimson-red object behind them, perhaps a new rug. His head swayed back and forth and side to side as he blinked to make out what the large mass was. His jaw dropped and his mouth opened. Could it be blood? There's no way—it was about the circumference of a pitcher's mound.

As the police officers moved toward him, he cocked his head in one direction and saw her. It was Cassie. She was on the floor by the large red puddle. He could see her face, with both her mouth and eyes open, staring not at him, but off into space. She didn't move an inch. She was right there with her arms outstretched and legs folded over each other. The large red glistening object was clearly a gigantic pool of blood, and she was lying motionless in the middle of it.

"No," he screamed at the top of his lungs as he darted toward her lifeless body. "No, no, no, no."

The two Seattle police officers wrapped their large arms around him, restraining him from getting any closer. "Sir, please come with us," one of them mustered. Conner's arms and entire body were flailing around, trying to reach out to her and touch her, all the while screaming over and over again, "No, no, no, no, no. It can't be. It can't beeeeeeeeeeeeeeeeeeeeee."

What he saw was the most horrific sight he had ever laid eyes on. The deep cuts in her skin were peeled away from each other and covered with blood. He could see gaping cuts in her neck, on her arms, and one that even traveled halfway up her cheek. Her eyes were wide open and milky. Her body was piled on top of itself, surrounded by dark red blood. He couldn't believe the amount of blood. How could such a small person produce that amount of blood?

"God, please no," Conner said and began to repeat that phrase over and over again. "Jesus. Please help me. Please, Jesus, help me. Please." The cops began to push him out of the apartment into the hallway. "The paramedics will be here soon," one of them reassured him.

Conner's mind was going faster than the speed of light. There were crackling sounds popping in his brain. He was feeling deep pain for her. He thought about her throat being cut and began to choke and gag. It felt like he was going to throw up. He urinated in his pants. He couldn't believe this was happening. "Please, wake up," he kept yelling. "Please, wake up," he said, praying to God that this was the worst and most vivid nightmare he had ever experienced. "Please let me in there. I want to see her."

As the paramedics passed him in the hall and entered the apartment several minutes later, he knew it was too late. There was no chance of resuscitation. No chance of reviving her. She was definitely dead.

"Sir?" one of the uniformed officers said. "What is your name, sir?"

"Conner," he said with a high-pitched squeal, as if he was just stuck in the stomach with a butcher knife. Tears streamed out of his bloodshot eyes and he began drooling onto the hardwood floor, banging the butt of his fist into the ground repeatedly. The neighbors began to come out of their apartments to see what was going on.

"Conner, the homicide detectives are on their way," the officer assured him with a gristly voice. "Are you her husband?"

"She is... she was my fiancée," Conner cried. *She was*, he thought. I'll never see her alive again. Please, God, please let this be a dream. Please tell me this is not really happening. He pressed his hands together tightly in prayer.

The emotional pain he felt was unbearable. It was physical pain. It was as if someone slowly gutted him with a chainsaw, removed his heart and his soul, and left him there for years and years, to bleed out like a frail husk of what was once a great man. The simultaneous feeling of shock and loss was completely overwhelming. He felt like every physical and emotional pain he had ever experienced over his lifetime had just been put into a vial and shot into his veins at a thousand different points all over his body.

The only thing he wanted that very moment was to die. He wished more than anything that he was lying in a pool of blood right beside her, free of this all-powerful assault of excruciating pain.

Conner tried to calm down, slowing his breathing and starting to shake more slowly. He kept saying "no, no, no, no," but this time under his breath. His body had slid down the wall and he was now crouched on the ground, rocking back and forth saying "no" over and over and over again. He thought about asking one of the officers for their gun so he could take his own life right then and there, changing his mind as logic took over. There was no way in hell they would offer him such an easy way out of this situation.

"She was everything to me," Conner finally said, glaring at the two officers with tears pouring down both cheeks. "Everything." Conner's eyes were puffy and his face was red. His hair stood up on end and he kept drawing his white knuckles through it aggressively.

The officers looked at each other, feeling for this poor soul. Even with all the blood, pain, and tragedy they saw on a daily basis, these officers were not so desensitized to recognize the indescribable hurt Conner felt. They both empathized with him.

"I'm really sorry, sir," one of the officers managed to say after a brief pause. Conner appreciated the gesture but knew there was nothing anyone could say to take away the anguish he felt in every neuron and every cell of his body.

The multitude of thoughts and feelings rushing through his head and heart began to slow down in intensity as well. The shock was subsiding, and Conner began to really grasp the gravity of the situation. He would never again look into those beautiful eyes. The frequent trysts with his sexual soul mate would be no more. There would be no more picnics or ball games, long talks. She would never again cook him wonderful dinners. He wouldn't ever be able to stare at her with disbelief that she was actually his. He would never be able to tell her how much he loved her ever again. Worst of all, he never got to say goodbye.

The pain began to deepen and spread. He had never experienced loss like this before. She was the person he had come to love more than any other human being on the planet, the wonderful woman to whom he could tell anything. The beautiful soul on whom he could lean if he was feeling down. She was gone forever. He remembered when his grandfather died. He'd sat in the family room at the hospital and clutched

Cassie, crying into her chest for what seemed like hours. She did nothing else but console him, running her fingers through his hair. And now she wasn't here to comfort him in his deepest time of intense sorrow. Because she was the one who was gone.

He began to shake uncontrollably. He futilely tried to focus on something else. Anything else. The ideas that were going through his head would only make him more and more depressed. He couldn't stand the thought of going through the rest of his life without her. The sadness he felt was unbearable. It was all he could think about. He would never see her again. The love of his life was no longer on this earth to tell him everything was going to be all right... because everything *wasn't* going to be all right. He would never look at the world the same way, full of hope and promise. He would never be the same again.

Conner thought one thing could bring him some modicum of comfort. The next chance he had to kill himself, he would immediately do it. Swallow a handful of pills. Slit his wrists. Hang himself. Jump off of a high-rise. He couldn't wait for that to happen. He would end his life like a Shakespearean tragedy. Offing himself at his first opportunity to spend the rest of eternity with the person he cherished more than anyone else in the universe. He was looking forward to that and finally had a good feeling travel quickly across a few of his synapses. All he wanted to do at this moment was die.

CHAPTER 13

Conner was taken downstairs and driven to the police station in a police car before the body was wheeled out on the gurney. The cops thought it would be better to not have him watch Cassie's body transported in a thick plastic body bag and add to his despair. They also brought him down some clean clothes so he wouldn't have to sit around all night in urine-soaked pants.

Once at the station, Conner had a long conversation with Detective Maury Stevens, the lead homicide investigator on the case. Conner stared straight ahead, never making eye contact with the detective.

The interview rooms in the station were both being used, so they adjourned to Maury Stevens's office, which was a complete mess. Conner was staring just over the seasoned detective's completely bald head and spotted an amalgam of file folders and criminal justice books crammed haphazardly into a metal bookshelf. Similarly, there was a random stack of file folders and papers strewn about on the detective's desk. Two cups of coffee in Styrofoam cups, one for Conner and one for Detective Stevens, were balanced on the stack of papers, precipitously enough that they could fall over at any moment. They both let off a steady stream of steam that flowed randomly up from the cups, twisting and turning a bit and then disappearing about two inches above their rims.

Conner averted his eyes from the bookshelf for a moment and looked Detective Stevens in the eyes, which were bloodshot, with dark brown centers. He was an overweight black gentleman, probably about 280 pounds. He wore black wireframe eyeglasses and his bald head and cheeks were speckled with dark freckles. To Conner, he looked to be about fifty, with deep wrinkles around his eyes. He squinted a lot. He was weathered and worn from his career of investigating gruesome homicides in the Seattle area and who knows where else.

Although Detective Stevens was speaking to Conner at length, Conner couldn't seem to concentrate. He couldn't stop thinking about his special Cassie. He would never have the pleasure of seeing her twist her hair, bite her lip, throw a concentrated look his way.

There was nothing he could do to bring her back. All he wanted was one more chance to see her. One more chance to hold her hand and feel the soft skin of her fingertips caress his palm.

The detective asked him several questions and Conner managed to eke out yes and no answers to most everything. Every once in a while, Conner would break down in tears. Some questions triggered overwhelming pain and agony. Every time he visualized his poor Cassie being murdered, he was overcome with devastating emotion and he completely lost it. At one point, he dropped to the musty wood floor and smacked it with his palm, screaming over and over again, "It's not fair. It's just so not fair. It's not fair." A dense, heavy rhythm echoed in the office.

The detective tried to comfort Conner by telling him they would do whatever was in their power to bring her killer to justice. *That's not going to bring her back,* Conner thought, feeling the pain of overwhelming loss cutting through his bones deeper and deeper with every passing moment.

Throughout the exchange with the detective, Conner was able to piece together the night's events in his mind. It turned out that the door was forced open and Cassie was attacked with a razor-sharp object. The initial observations pointed to her attacker using a short knife, like a scalpel. Conner couldn't understand how a person could do such a thing. How could anyone take a small, sharp object and slice another human being to death with it? What would possess them to do that? How could they have no feelings while they viciously attacked her? How long did it take her to die? Didn't they know her parents and loved ones would miss her?

Conner began to drift off, unintentionally ignoring Detective Stevens's statements and questions. He started to think about what happened to poor Cassie, struggling with all her might to save her life, calling Conner's name for help. What were her last words? How did she try to fight off her attacker?

Her attacker. With all of the emotional turmoil, this hadn't even crossed his mind until this very moment. Conner knew exactly who her killer was. It had to be. A small sharp object. The potential sighting of this person weeks before. There was no other explanation. He was sure of it. It was Seth.

CHAPTER 14

"Conner. Conner. Conner." Detective Stevens finally yelled to get Conner's attention. "It's obvious that you are in no condition to answer my questions tonight. I've asked you several things and you've been unable to answer me or you simply give me a blank stare," Stevens stated. "Now, I understand that you're going through a lot right now..."

If you only knew, Conner pondered. *If you only knew.*

"But, please," Stevens urged with increasing intensity. "I have one very important question to ask you that I need to know right away because it is critical to act quickly when investigating crimes like this."

Conner finally perked up. He sat up in his chair and looked into the middle-aged detective's spectacles. "Yes, sir?" Conner said.

"Do you have any idea who would have done this?" Stevens quickly asked. "Did Cassie have any enemies, or people who have hurt her in the past?"

Conner looked up to the ceiling. He struggled to keep his composure. After wiping some salty tears away from his eyes and taking another sip of his coffee, he uttered, "No."

He looked away from his now steamless coffee cup, stared at Detective Stevens right in his blackish eyes, and followed with, "I have no idea who on earth would do such a horrible thing to her."

It immediately became clear what he needed to do. With all the pain, all of the feelings of loss, injustice, and hatred, he devised a plan. Instead of blurting out who the most likely suspect was, he was going to kill Seth Warner. It had to be him, with the murder weapon, the past threats, the potential sighting... it became painfully obvious who the perpetrator was.

If he gave the police his name, it might take days, weeks, or months for them to find him. And if he decided to stand trial, that could take several weeks or months as well. If he was found guilty, they would either sentence him to life in prison or some lesser sentence because Washington State had abolished the death penalty.

Conner wanted something swifter. No matter what it took, he was going to find him and he was going to kill him. He vowed to do whatever he could to find Seth Warner and murder him before the police found him.

Detective Stevens squinted even further, a seemingly impossible task due to the permanent wrinkles that cracked the space from the edges of his eyes to his temples. He wasn't necessarily questioning the truth of Conner's statement. Just waiting. Detective Stevens had always found that when it came to premeditated murders, people could usually find someone in the person's past who would want to do them harm. All they had to do was think about it for a few seconds. Additionally, when people are brutally murdered like this, experience told Stevens that it was usually someone the person knew, especially in cases where no property was taken from the house. Detective Stevens was convinced it was a premeditated act. Typically, people who murder strangers randomly do not slice up their victims so viciously. They don't cut their face. They don't make them suffer. Random acts of violence, in Stevens's experience, were more impersonal and could even be described as efficient.

Although Stevens was convinced that if he waited several seconds, someone's name would come to Conner's mind, no one's did.

Conner's mind started racing a million miles an hour. Thoughts started darting back and forth at breakneck speed. None of those thoughts bubbled up into speech. He began looking around the room, unable to focus on anything.

Stevens modified the question into an open-ended one. "Who might be able to commit such an unspeakable act?" Still, nothing came out of Conner's mouth.

Detective Stevens decided to reschedule the interview with Conner for the next day. While the information wouldn't be as fresh in his mind, Stevens thought it better to give the poor guy a break and talk to him again when he was calmer and the wounds weren't so fresh.

"Do you have someone to stay with for the next few days?" Detective Stevens asked. "We recommend that you not return to your apartment until we've had time to complete our investigation and clea—"

Stevens paused mid-word. Conner knew exactly what he was talking about. They had to clean the pool of blood the circumference of a pitcher's mound before Conner returned to his apartment. Stevens also knew that a variety of people would have to come through the apartment, including more detectives, criminalists from forensics, and reps from the district attorney's office and the medical examiner's office. The investigation was far from over.

Sensing Detective Stevens's discomfort, Conner picked up the conversation at the break. "Yes, Detective, my brother Joseph. He's waiting down in the lobby for me."

Conner scheduled a follow-up interview for 10:00 a.m. the next day to finish the interview and provide further information to the detective. Before Conner left, he assured Detective Stevens that he would cooperate in any way he could to make sure they found the person who had done this, and that he appreciated all of their time and effort.

As he made his way down the elevator, Conner began to think about his answer to the critically important question that Detective Stevens asked at the end of the interview. *What are you doing? You're not a murderer. You can't do this. You should just tell them about Seth tomorrow. Let the authorities handle this.*

The elevator door opened and he spotted Joseph, who rose and quickly headed toward Conner as he limped sheepishly out of the elevator. Joseph jogged toward the emotionally injured man who was once his brother and engulfed him in a powerful embrace. They both began bawling.

CHAPTER 15

Conner didn't sleep at all that night. He tossed and turned in his brother's guest room, wishing there was something he could have done to save Cassie's life. If only he was there an hour earlier. Maybe he would have arrived at the right time to stop the murder. He was disturbed by the visualizations he couldn't get out of his head, about Cassie's murder, and he was searching for any relief for his feelings of loss.

Conner hoped that he would wake up the next day and find that it had all been a dream, or maybe an extremely vivid hallucination. Maybe he got a bad case of food poisoning from the coleslaw he ate at lunch and he was laid up in a hospital bed with a high fever and poison-induced hallucinations haunting his brain. In this case, he was briefly comforted by the thought of his precious Cassie sitting by his hospital bedside, clutching his hand as he thrashed around as a result of these horrific visions.

Conner saw the sunrise and thought he might have dozed off for a couple of hours, but he still felt extremely fuzzy. He rolled out of his brother's bed and ambled down the hallway, finding his brother moping around the kitchen. Conner saw coffee grounds scattered around the counter, and his brother fumbled with a coffee filter. He obviously didn't make coffee at home much, but he owned a coffee maker for guests and relatives who stayed over at his house. Joseph stopped immediately and shot an empathetic look toward his shattered brother.

"What... what happened last night?" Conner cried out. His brother darted toward Conner and caught him as his body buckled and nearly fell to the ground. Joseph caught his frail brother with his strong arms and propped him up as they both began crying again. "I'm so sorry, Conner. I can't tell you how sorry I am," Joseph yelled as he tried in vain to hold back his tears and control his emotions, thinking he should demonstrate strength because Conner had obviously lost his.

Conner then realized that this was not a dream or hallucination. Cassie was dead, and there was nothing he could do about it. The pain began to deepen, and Conner felt his consciousness begin to fade in and out. His soul began to splinter. This once strong person with a powerful personality and an infinite amount of love in his heart was irreparably ruptured. He hated the thoughts that wouldn't leave his head. He would have to go through the rest of his life without the person that perfectly complemented him. He would never again love another person the way he loved his sweet Cassie.

After clumsily brewing a half pot of coffee and serving Conner a couple of cups, which Conner cried into more than drank, Conner begrudgingly readied himself for his 10:00 a.m. appointment at the police station.

CHAPTER 16

As Conner rode to the police station in his brother's VW Bus, he thought about whether he should identify Cassie's potential attacker. What if he delayed their efforts and they were not able to find Seth? Was he prepared to exact vigilante revenge on Cassie's murderer? In the end, Conner wanted Seth Warner to feel the pain that Conner felt, and a jail cell wouldn't have the same effect as a slow, painful, torturous death.

As the VW Bus screeched to a halt in the parking garage of the police station, Conner jerked open the creaky door and accompanied his brother toward the entrance of the police station.

Although Conner was in better shape than he had been the previous night, he provided little or no help to the investigating detective. Conner answered every question Detective Stevens asked, but he gave him little to go on. Conner reconstructed the last few days of her life and provided details about Cassie's daily routine. He talked about her friends, her family life, and their wedding plans. But he didn't volunteer any information about her potentially dangerous ex-boyfriend.

Detective Stevens was convinced Conner didn't have any idea who the murderer was. The hardened detective figured that if Conner had any leads, he would tell the detective right away so her killer could be brought to justice. Conner cringed a few times as Stevens referred to the crime scene and the assumed murder weapon, but he mostly maintained his composure. His pain and emotional turmoil began to give way to numbness, and he eventually started to answer the questions in a cold, calculated manner, as if he had the words memorized from a script. The detective dismissed Conner after an hour and a half of questions and discussions, and Conner was escorted back to the VW Bus by his brother.

After traveling back to Joseph's house, Conner plopped himself down on the couch and turned on the TV, trying to find a program that would distract him from the pain and loss he was feeling. He desperately searched for something that would take his mind off the fact that he'd lost Cassie forever.

As Conner drifted off to sleep in front of the TV, with his brother close by, Conner began to think about his plot to find Seth Warner and end the life of this mentally disturbed man. As the dark clouds in his brain began to lift as a result of the mental and physical exhaustion setting in, he realized that he was fully committed to this plan. He didn't want the slow and lumbering criminal justice system led by Detective Stevens to bring the killer to justice. Conner wanted revenge. And he thought he had everything he needed to get it.

CHAPTER 17

Conner woke up in the middle of the night, blinking his puffy eyes and finally focusing on the window, which was being pelted by bullet-size raindrops. As he sat up and pressed his palms against his closed eyes, Conner continued to process all that had happened. His life would never be the same. He would never look at the world the same way again. Something would always be missing.

He figured he had everything he needed to accomplish the daunting task of exacting revenge on Seth. Conner knew the person who killed his lover. He knew that he went to WSU. He knew that he may have recently been in the Seattle area, so there must be some evidence that he could follow. These clues would lead him to Cassie's attacker. But how could he get this done? What weapon would he use, and where would he get it? He didn't have any experience tracking someone down. He wouldn't even know where to start. Conner realized that he would have to get some professional assistance.

As these questions and obstacles began to gnash in and out of Conner's thoughts, he noticed his pain and feelings of loss begin to dissipate. He found the feeling of devastating suffering going away. It was being replaced by vivid fantasies of exacting revenge on Cassie's murderer. He thought about slashing Seth Warner's throat, watching the blood spurt out of the fresh wound. Conner felt the pain lessen more and more, and it was replaced by a very strange and unfamiliar feeling—pleasure. He even found himself giggling quietly as he pictured Seth begging for his life. Even though Conner didn't know what he looked like, he pictured a tall, brown-haired figure with a square jaw, spitting up blood and looking up at Conner with terror and fear.

Conner blinked and shook his head hard. *Are you out of your mind?* he thought. There was no way he could take someone else's life. He couldn't kill another human being. Conner turned and laid flat on the couch. He stared at the ceiling, laying his forearm on his forehead, listening to the raindrops hitting the window like a gentle tommy gun. "This isn't the answer," Conner whispered to himself under his breath. "You need to call Detective Stevens tomorrow and tell him the truth. You know who did this, and you need to tell the authorities." Conner knew this was the right thing to do, but he was unsure he could do it.

The only thought that pushed the overwhelming feelings of despair and anguish away were the gruesome depictions of Conner exacting vengeance on Cassie's killer. Conner thought through his dilemma for a few more hours and didn't come to any resolution. *I'll figure this out tomorrow,* Conner thought. *Get some sleep,* he commanded. As he drifted off, he was plagued with the visuals of the murder scene. He wanted more than anything to take Cassie's pain away. He prayed to God that she went unconscious right away and didn't have to deal with the pain and terror of being violently murdered.

CHAPTER 18

The police pursued several leads over the next few days, including a suspected serial killer who was still at large. This mysterious killer had victimized several women in the Seattle area within the prior months. The authorities determined this lead to be a dead end largely because the murder with a short, sharp object didn't fit the profile of the other serial killer, who preferred strangulation. The police even briefly investigated Conner himself due to the fact that many murder victims are killed by people who are closest to them. However, Conner had a bulletproof alibi with the school superintendent presentation, with several witnesses who corroborated his whereabouts.

Conner wasn't worried about the investigation. He mustered enough energy to bring himself to go to the funeral, and he found himself looking at Cassie's casket as it was lowered into her grave. Conner started crying from the moment he arrived at the cemetery.

It was a clear day, no rain, very few cumulus clouds in the sky. Conner wished it was pissing rain, pelting him from all angles, a typical Seattle day. That would have been a more appropriate climate for this particular event. But, no, the birds were chirping louder than ever, the sun blanketed the earth, Mother Nature was happy. It was unbecoming weather for the weight of this event.

He couldn't bear to look at Cassie's parents, who were weeping about twenty feet away from him. He saw the minister and glanced at him a few times, but he wasn't hearing what he said. Conner's mind raced, and his mourning began to intensify.

"Though as I walk through the valley of the shadow of death, I shall fear no evil," the nameless minister orated. Conner tuned the rest out.

As Conner was heading for one of the dozens of limos, Cassie's mother, Amy, approached Conner. They embraced and she whispered in his ear.

"How could have this happened?" Amy said.

Conner pulled his arm up and wiped his tears, and he began crying even harder.

"I have no idea." Conner coughed. "I'm so, so sorry."

The two loosened their embrace and began wandering toward their respective vehicles. Conner brought his hands to his face, drying as many tears as he could. Just then, Joseph came from the side and wrapped his arm around Conner's neck. "I love you, buddy," Joseph said in a deep gravely tone. "I'm so sorry for your loss."

While in the limo, Conner felt a buzzing in his pocket. He picked up his phone and saw an unknown number with a Seattle area code.

Flipping it to his ear, he barked, "Hello."

"Hey, Conner, it's Stevens. Just wanted to give you an update," Stevens said.

Conner propped himself up. Maybe there was a break in the case. Perhaps they found Seth. His mind started racing again.

"So, we have been unable to identify any suspects. We haven't found anyone with the motive and ability to carry out the attack, but we're still looking," Stevens stressed. "However, this case will remain open, and any new leads or developments will be brought to your attention right away."

Conner took a deep breath. "All right, thank you, Mr. Stevens. Let me know if anything else turns up," he said in a somber tone.

After Conner pushed the "END" button on his cell phone, he sighed and entered the detective's phone number into his contact list. He sank back into the leather seat of the limousine and felt relief. Conner's investigation had only begun.

CHAPTER 19

Conner knew he would need help with this delicate operation. He couldn't possibly hope to track down the suspect
by himself, so he decided he needed professional help. He
jumped online one morning after Joseph went to work and
Googled "private investigators Seattle."

Dozens of records were returned as a result of his search.
Conner scanned a few websites and decided on a private
investigator named Bob Gannet. Gannet was a former police detective with more than thirty years of experience. His
specialty was missing persons as well as adoptee investigations—people who were looking to find children they gave
up for adoption years before.

In addition, Gannet's website explained he also investigated infidelity and insurance fraud. He thought it was nice that
Mr. Gannet had such broad-based experience.

Conner picked up the phone and called Bob Gannet Investigations. A raspy-voiced woman answered the phone.

"Bob Gannet Investigations, how may I help you?" she
choked.

"Uh, hi. I'd like to talk to Mr. Gannet, please."

"What is it regarding?" The receptionist obviously said this about seventeen times a day, based on her robotic delivery.

Conner cleared his throat. "Hmmm-mmpph. I'd like to talk to him about hiring him for a job."

"One moment, please." The receptionist hammered the phone with her finger and transferred the call. After a brief moment on hold, listening to the most unbearable merengue music, the phone picked up.

"Gannet here," a high-pitched voice said.

"Hello. My name's Conner, and I wanted to see if you could help me find someone," Conner explained.

"Is it a missing person or relative?" the high-pitch voice inquired.

"Uh, neither. It's an old friend from college."

"Have you tried Facebook?" Gannet chuckled.

"I've tried Facebook, LinkedIn, Instagram, and even Twitter. Based on my initial research, I think it might be a little more difficult task than that," Conner said sternly.

"OK, can you tell me about this person?" Gannet said briskly.

Conner paused. "Well, is there any way we could meet in person to talk about this?"

Mr. Gannet silently shook his head. He was very familiar with people not wanting to discuss sensitive issues over the phone. It went with the territory when dealing with people who were mostly paranoid about any authorities listening in or calls being recorded.

"I have some time tomorrow afternoon. Where would you like to meet?" Gannet took a pack of Tic Tacs and drank down three or four of them.

"Where are you located?" Conner said enthusiastically.

Gannet shot back, "I'm right near Discovery Park."

Conner pondered this for a second. "OK, I could meet you during my lunch break, but I only have forty-five minutes. Could we meet halfway?"

"Sure, kid, what did you have in mind?" Gannet queried.

"How about Kerry Park? By the Changing Form sculpture?" Conner shot back quickly, remembering that his first kiss with Cassie had been at that exact location.

"Whatever you say, pal," Gannet squeaked. "Two o'clock?"

"Works for me," Conner said in an upbeat tone. "See you then. Thanks."

"OK, bye," Gannet said before slamming down the phone receiver and taking another chug of wintergreen Tic Tacs.

CHAPTER 20

With an expected life insurance settlement of nearly $300,000, Conner would have no problem affording this private investigator, though he wondered what the final cost would be. Was it going to be a flat fee or an hourly arrangement? How long would it take to find Seth Warner? What would the final bill be? Would this all be kept confidential?

Conner had more questions than answers, but he figured he'd get all of his questions answered by the squeaky-voiced PI.

As he drove to the park to meet Mr. Gannet in the afternoon, he began to think about his first kiss with Cassie at the Changing Form sculpture, which looked like large steel cubes with ovals in the middle, stacked on top of each other. It was during their first date, after a lovely meal in Seattle at Betty Restaurant and Bar. The couple had walked through the park, talking about their appreciation for art. Conner, being more of the artistic type, spoke in detail about how the sculpture made him feel. When he found that he was at a loss for words, Cassie looked at him seductively, pulled him close by his jacket, and planted a soft kiss on his lips. Conner was really nervous and didn't think he'd get a kiss at the end of the night for no real reason. Cassie was such a good kisser. Her lips were so soft and gentle, and his lips went from trembling to calm within a few seconds. He remembered having a moment of elation and excitement after the kiss that didn't go away for hours. He took the kiss as a good sign that he'd earned a second date, and he did, and so much more than that.

Conner snapped out of his daydream just in time to arrive at the park and make his way up to the sculpture. He used the memory of the first kiss as his justification that this was the right thing. That his exacting vengeance on Cassie's killer would fill the holes in Conner's heart, holes that were larger than the ones in the sculpture. He foresaw these gaps growing even larger over the coming years.

As he began to scale the hill where the Changing Form sculpture resided, Conner began to rehearse the conversation with Mr. Gannet. He wanted to make sure he didn't incriminate himself because he assumed a private investigator could not obtain information that could be used for the commission of a crime.

Once Conner arrived at the sculpture, he cupped his hands and blew into them to stave off the cold. During wintertime, his hands turned extremely dry, forcing him to apply lotion quite frequently. Today, though, he hadn't applied any lotion so his hands were severely chapped. He glanced at his hands and then rubbed them together, hoping to shed some of the dead skin.

"Conner," a voice said behind him.

"That's me," Conner said instinctively. "How did you know it was... ?"

"I locate people for a living. I would be really bad at my job if I couldn't find you," Gannet said.

Not knowing if he was making a joke or delivering a truly awkward sales pitch, Conner let out a high-pitched grunt, hoping Gannet would interpret it as either a laugh or a verbal agreement. Gannet was a seasoned detective, and he was well aware that Conner was related to an unsolved murder a few weeks ago, and he was already connecting the dots.

"So, tell me about this person you're looking for," Gannet said in a grisly tone. "I understand it's an old friend from college."

"That's right," Conner said, being sure to choose his words wisely. "His name is Seth Warner, and he graduated in 2004 from Washington State. I understand that he moved back East, but I believe he might be in town."

Gannet casually flipped open a Moleskine notebook and started scribbling furiously. "You said he moved back East. Do you know what city or state?"

Conner looked down while squeezing his lips and sighed a little. "I really don't, I could give you some guesses, but they would be just that, guesses and speculation."

"What makes you think he's in town?" Gannet quizzed.

"A mutual friend mentioned seeing him. He couldn't be 100 percent sure, but he seemed pretty confident."

"All right, well, do you have any idea where he could be staying? Do you know when he may be leaving Seattle?" Gannet said, motioning to Conner to sit at a nearby bench.

"I don't know that information; I'm really sorry," Conner mustered.

"Why are you looking to reconnect with this person?" Gannet shot back, squinting one eye as he poked his tongue with his old-school Bic pen.

"I haven't seen him in a while. I just think it would be good to get in touch and have dinner or some drinks," Conner said as his mind started racing. "We were really close, but then lost touch, so I want to see if we can reconnect."

Gannet licked his lips and snuck his notebook into his jacket pocket.

"My typical fee for finding a person is $150 per hour. I will spend ten hours searching for the person, and if they aren't found at that point, we can discuss whether we allocate another block of hours or just go our separate ways."

"Do you take personal checks?" Conner shot back at lightning speed.

Gannet took a breath and leaned back into the bench. "Sure thing, buddy. Sure thing. Make it out to Bob Gannet Investigations, Gannet has two *N*s, one *T*."

After a deep pause, Gannet said in a booming voice, "You really want to get in touch with this guy, don't you?"

"Yes, I do," Conner said confidently. "Yes, I do." Conner looked down to make the check out on his left knee.

Gannet leaned over. "If you want you can pay me half now..."

"No need. I'll just cut you a check for the full amount. It will be easier for both of us."

After exchanging contact information, Conner and Gannet rose from the bench, Gannet with a deep grunt, then they said goodbye with a firm handshake and a look of agreement. They both stutter-stepped a few times down the hill on their way out of the park.

CHAPTER 21

The first day back at the apartment was a gut-wrenching experience. All Conner could think of was an exaggerated pool of blood that could easily fill a bathtub. The volume of blood grew and grew and grew in his mind as he continued to recall the traumatic event. Even though the blood was miraculously cleaned up, no trace left, Conner could see it in his memory and couldn't take his mind off it.

As he wandered around and surveyed the apartment, he started to well up. The emptiness and coldness of the apartment reminded him that he would never again see the love of his life. He imagined her dicing some mushrooms on the cutting board, reading in bed, or just mundanely watching TV. And he knew he would never again find true, unconditional love like hers.

His tears quickly turned into sobs and, before too long, he was kneeling by the bed with the upper part of his body lying flat on the bed, crying and pounding, crying and pounding.

"Why, God, why? Whyyyyyyyy, God, whyyyyyyy?"

After twenty minutes, Conner fell over and curled up into a fetal position. A combination of tears and saliva formed a puddle underneath his cheek as he passed out.

Bzzzzzzzzzzz. Bzzzzzzzzzzz. Bzzzzzzzzzzz. Bzzzzzzzzzzz.

Conner realized his phone was ringing. He rolled onto his butt and fished the phone out of his pocket. It was Joseph.

"Hey, dude," Conner hissed with a raspy voice.

"Hi, buddy. How's the first day at the apartment?" Joseph asked with genuine concern.

"Uh, it's fine," Conner said, knowing he was lying through his teeth. He started to sniffle and cough as he woke himself up.

"Really?" Joseph retorted with a skeptical tone.

Conner paused, knowing that he'd been caught in a lie. "Actually, it's pretty fucking horrible. What are you up to?"

"Just getting ready to grab some sushi," Joseph answered.

Conner knew what Joseph was doing. He knew full well that Conner's favorite sushi joint was mere minutes by foot, and he could easily be talked into dinner there.

Conner wanted to say no. He wanted to go back to sleep and forget the horrific act that had been committed mere weeks ago. But he also knew his brother was deeply concerned about him and wanted to make sure everything was cool.

"You thinking Shiki?" Conner said, trying to feign excitement.

"Uh-huh. Does that work for you?" Joseph casually asked.

"Sure. I'll see you there at seven," Conner said while pressing "END" on his cell phone.

After jumping in the shower and putting on some clean clothes, Conner walked swiftly to the door, averting his gaze from where the blood pond had been, flung the door open, slammed it shut, and locked it.

The brisk walk to Shiki Japanese restaurant on Roy Street was just as short as Conner remembered. He made it in four minutes flat from door to door. By the time he arrived, Joseph already had a table, which was odd, considering he was chronically late.

"Hey, bro, I already ordered the deep-fried oysters," Joseph volunteered gently.

"Thanks, man, you're acting really nice right now. Are you going to ask me for a big favor or something?" Conner asked this surprisingly playfully, considering his mood merely an hour before.

"Naw, Conner. I just know how difficult today must be for you..." Joseph trailed off as he said this.

"It's actually not that bad. I had a tough time at first, but it's pretty much back to normal. Signs of a struggle are gone. There's no more bloo..."

"Do you need to stay with me longer?" Joseph offered. "I don't mind at all. I just want to make sure your head's straight before you start assimilating back into society."

"I'll be fine," Conner said with contempt. "At some point, I have to rip the Band-Aid off. What better time than now?"

"OK, good. Do you want me to stay over?" Joseph said softly.

"No, thanks. Like I said, rip off the Band-Aid," Conner said while motioning to his arm and pantomiming tearing a Band-Aid off.

Joseph and Conner spent the rest of dinner mostly silent. They wolfed down spicy tuna rolls, uni, and eel, and drank a few glasses of Japanese beer.

After parting ways with a big hug and many loud pats, Conner began walking home just as it started to rain. He jogged most of the way, making an eight-minute walk into a three-and-a-half-minute run. He took the elevator upstairs and unlocked the door. As he pushed the door in, he said a little prayer asking God to return his sweet Cassie. He wanted her to miraculously appear on the couch when he opened the door, maybe in the bathroom taking a shower. He prayed this had been the most vivid and terrifying dream ever. Maybe he would wake up in the hospital out of a coma and discover that this had just been a psychotic delusion.

The door opened with a crunch, and it was the same empty apartment he had left two hours ago. No Cassie, no delusion, no blood puddle.

Conner's heart jumped. He was determined to escape thinking about Cassie's horrific death. It was time to start planning Seth Warner's death. He sat down at his desk and peeled off a piece of paper and grabbed a pen. He started sketching out how he would do it. He would find Seth and he would shoot him, as simple as that. As much as he would love to slice him up with an X-Acto knife, he determined it would be too impractical and dangerous. If Seth wrestled the implement away from Conner, he could turn the tables and attack Conner. That obviously wouldn't do.

It was obvious he would have to use a gun. It would be relatively easy to get and easy to hide, and it could end Seth's life with the squeeze of the trigger. He could walk up to Seth on the street or in some other place and blow his brains out. Or perhaps he would shoot him in the stomach, then tell him why he was dying as he gurgled blood and clutched his gut. Then he could shoot him square in the head to make absolutely sure he died once and for all.

Conner started running through these scenarios in his head and he brightened up. He was smiling and biting his bottom lip with excitement. The prospect of killing his lover's murderer gave him a rush of exhilaration. He felt the adrenaline flowing through his veins and laid back into his chair, enjoying this dopamine-driven state.

After laying out his loose plan of attack on paper, Conner realized that he had to get something and get something quick.

Conner needed to buy a gun.

CHAPTER 22

"The fuck you need a gun for, Archie?" Michael asked him while tilting his head and giving him a goofy, crazy look with the eye that wasn't lazy.

"Have you ever heard of the concept of 'no questions asked'?" Conner said with confidence, starting to get a bit nervous and feeling his heartbeat grow more intense in power and in frequency. Conner wasn't in the best neighborhood, and he glanced around quickly to survey his environment.

"A'ight, man," Michael said as he shook his head, realizing the gun wasn't going to be used to make this guy feel safer at night, but rather for something violent. "I can give you a Glock for $200 or a deuce deuce for $100."

"I definitely need something a little more powerful than a deuce deuce," Conner said seriously. "Is the Glock like a nine millimeter or a forty-five caliber or what?" It was painfully clear to Michael that Conner knew little to nothing about guns.

Michael rolled his eye. "It's a nine," he said, sounding slightly annoyed. He looked around to make sure no one overheard their conversation. "I gotta TEC-9 if that would do better for ya."

"That's a little *too* much firepower," Conner said in all seriousness, remembering that was one of the guns the Columbine shooters used. "Needs to be handheld and easy to hide." Conner began to get more and more nervous the more he talked about the impending firearm purchase.

"I'll take a Glock," Conner said in a softer tone of voice, reaching into his left pocket, in which he had two crisp $100 bills. He had $300 in his right pocket, just in case it was more. He planned this process to be as efficient as possible.

"Hang on," Michael said as he strutted back to the alley, grabbing a black metal item from the channel on the side of the dumpster.

Michael motioned for Conner to join him in the alley. Conner froze. His heart was beating out of his chest, and he began to hyperventilate. What if this guy wanted to rob him? He obviously knew he had cash on him. Thinking better of it, he mustered as much confidence as he could and ambled into the alleyway, passed Michael the two bills, and took the gun out of Michael's hand by the handle.

"Do you have any ammo?" Conner inquired.

Michael nodded. "It's loaded with hollow points. Let me grab you another clip with another fifteen in there."

Michael casually passed the other magazine to Conner. He looked deep into his eyes, knowing full well that someone was surely going to die. "This is free. Good luck," he said without even a tinge of emotion in his voice.

"Thanks, man," Conner quickly responded as he quickly averted his eyes, tucked the gun and magazine into his inside coat pocket, and started walking toward the sidewalk.

CHAPTER 23

Conner stayed up until 3:00 a.m., playing with his new toy. He watched several videos on how to use the gun. He wanted to make sure he left nothing up to chance. He even went to a shooting range the next day to get comfortable shooting his new weapon. He sought training from the range attendant to adopt a better grip and refine his technique.

As he squeezed the trigger, his arm bounced back because of the recoil. He made sure to train his arm toward the exact same spot on the target, thinking of when the event would happen, he wanted to make sure to hit the target dead-on, taking no chances.

The feeling of pure elation Conner felt while planning Seth Warner's murder returned in full force. The elation washed over him and gave him a calm warm feeling inside. As the euphoric feeling flushed throughout his mind and body, he started to smile and smirk with each squeeze of the trigger. The smoke from the gunpowder traveled quickly to his nostrils and he was pleased with the smell. He unloaded the fifteen-round magazine with precision. *POP, POP, POP, POP, POP, POP.*

After getting home from the gun club, Conner ran to the bed and jumped into it. The rush from shooting the gun and shredding through paper targets wore him out. He crawled under the covers and clutched his knees, taking deep breaths to calm his excitement for what was to come.

Conner dreamed that night of viciously murdering Seth Warner. Visions of a bullet going into Seth's head filled his mind. He became Michael Corleone from *The Godfather*, shooting the two men in the restaurant. He was shooting his fiancée's murderer, first in the throat, so he could enjoy seeing Seth clutch his neck, unable to breathe. Maybe even in the gut so he would keel over in anguish. Soon after, Conner lifted the gun slightly, squeezing the trigger and watching the bullet enter his victim's head, blowing the back of his head out, and watching the red matter decorate the wall behind him. Conner was never a violent person, but this was giving him an insane amount of pleasure, he was enjoying these murderous fantasies.

"Cassie," Conner called out as his eyes blinked awake. He turned his attention to the extreme pain she had no doubt experienced prior to her murder. He kept projecting himself there, wondering if she knew who her attacker was, how she must have felt knowing her life was about to end.

For the rest of the night, Conner slept dreamless but erupted into a wakened state as he experienced phantom pains, which felt like a short, sharp knife gouging his neck, head, and chest. This manifested as imageless dreams, only feeling pain and anguish in a similar way that Cassie did. He woke up and tried to pray and wish these episodes away, hoping upon hope that these experiences would go away.

CHAPTER 24

Bzzzzzzzzzzz. Bzzzzzzzzzzz. Bzzzzzzzzzzz. Bzzzzzzzzzzz.
Conner slowly pried open his eyes and looked at his buzzing phone. He squinted, and as his eyes fluttered open and then closed, he was able to make out the name on the screen: Bob Gannet.

Conner lunged at the phone and knocked his alarm clock off the nightstand in the process. He slid his finger over the screen, but the call dropped. It was too late.

Conner snorted, swung his knees out and planted them squarely on the floor, and rubbed his nose with the butt of his palm. He knew Bob would either call back or leave a message, so he didn't call back right away. After counting from one Mississippi to twenty Mississippi, Conner hit Bob Gannet's name on his phone and it began to ring.

As the phone rang, Conner's thoughts darted around rapidly. Did he find Seth? Was he still in Seattle? Did he have any leads? Did he call because all he found were dead ends? Conner was anxious with excitement and nervous about the possibility that he hadn't found him.

"Hello," Bob choked out with more of a grizzled voice than usual.

"Hey, Bob, it's Conner. I saw you called. Do you have any information for me?" Conner delivered this quickly, so much so that Bob didn't understand half of the words, but he obviously got the idea.

"Yeah, I just wanted to call you and give you some news." Bob's voice trailed off. He then coughed, took a deep, labored breath and said, "I found him."

"You found him?" Conner shrieked with excitement, incredulous over what he'd expected to be an almost impossible task. "How did you find him?"

Bob chuckled in an almost Santa Claus manner. "Trade secrets, my boy, trade secrets. So, do you want to set up a time to meet so I can show you what I've found?"

"Absolutely," Conner shot back quicker than a machine gun. "Can we meet at Caffe Ladro on Roy Street and Queen Anne?"

"Huh, huh, huh," Bob belly laughed, acknowledging his youthful exuberance. "No problem. When do you want to mee—"

"Does 11:00 a.m. today work?" Conner urgently asked.

"Uh, I have a few meetings this morning. Will 2:00 p.m. work?" Bob took another raspy breath and exhaled through his nose.

Conner clenched his teeth, wanting to know what he found.

"I... I guess that's OK," Conner said with a defeated tone. "I'll see you then." He slowly pressed the "END" button on his phone.

As Conner unfolded back onto the bed and slapped the pillow with his head, his mind began to wander. What was good ole Bob Gannet able to unearth? Conner prayed he would give him some actionable information—say, a location where this psychopath would be in the next few days. He would love to know where he was staying so he could stake out the place. Then run up with guns blazing as he entered the door. As he began to think about what possibilities Gannet would bring to the table for Conner, he dozed off, sleeping for two additional hours.

CHAPTER 25

Conner walked briskly as he approached the coffeehouse. He had a single focus. No one was going to stop him. He wanted to find Seth Warner and kill him. He was going to take extra care to ensure Seth knew why he was dying and by whose hand.

As he turned the corner, he saw Bob Gannet, who was sitting outside with an espresso-size demitasse in front of him.

Conner zipped by the table. "I'll be right back, don't move," he said just before he walked into the café.

After grabbing his latte in a to-go cup, Conner cut right through the line that had accumulated after him and sat down across from Bob Gannet.

"So," Conner queried. "What'd you find out?"

"Well, you'll be happy to know that I found out a lot," Bob assured Conner. "Let me start from the beginning. We know he is only here temporarily. If you want to see him, you have about a three-week window."

"Tell me more. What else do you know about him?" Conner said with increased intensity.

Bob continued, "Well, he's staying in the city. He's flying back out to New York at the end of the month. Oh, he has a sister that lives here. Her name is..."

"Where is he staying?" Conner shouted. He wanted to know where he was right away. He was already excited about going there immediately to avenge Cassie's death. He wanted to make sure nothing got in the way of his murder.

Befuddled, Bob told him more about his research. "He's staying with his sister. He seems to be very close to her. He's actually having dinner with her on Friday night."

"Friday night?" Conner exclaimed. "What time? Where?"

Bob coughed a couple of times, licked his thumb, and fingered through his notes and read them off. "Looks like 7:00 p.m. at the Red Cow."

"Red Cow?" Conner again questioned. "I think that's over by Lake Washington. That will work perfect for my... er... surprise."

"Great. Is there anything else you need?" Bob offered.

"Uh... I don't think so," Conner said. "Oh, wait. Do you have any photos of him? It's... um... been a while since I've seen him."

Bob again paged through the notes in his dark brown file folder and offered a stack of photographs to Conner. "Sure, here you go."

When Conner saw Seth Warner, his face flushed, he started breathing heavily, and his heart started beating rapidly. Hatred was all he felt as he stared at the elusive murderer. Seth appeared to be tall, even taller than Conner, at six feet five or so. He was good looking. Broad shoulders, handsome face, big brown eyes, and thin lips. Conner couldn't help but notice how full his eyebrows were. His arms were defined and had visible veins, as though he was flexing in a fitness competition. Not what you'd think a cold-blooded murderer would look like.

Conner closed his eyes, taking mental snapshots of Seth's face and body to memorize them. He wanted to make completely sure he targeted and terminated the man who so callously killed his dear fiancée Cassie. He began to instinctively squeeze the sides of the pictures, wanting to crumble them up and rip them to shreds. Carefully, he loosened his grip on the photos and shoved the stack under his left armpit.

"I can't tell you how much I appreciate you tracking him down," Conner mentioned meekly. "This is better than I ever could have expected."

"No problem at all," Gannet wheezed. "That's why they pay me the big bucks."

Conner nodded and pursed his lips. "I gotcha. I can wholeheartedly say that I got my money's worth."

"Great. Just remember us if you need any other private investigator services," the portly, wrinkled man gargled.

"I sure will. Well, thanks again. I'll get in touch if I need anything else. Bye." Conner grabbed his latte, clutched the photos and papers Gannet gave him, and took off toward his house, excited to start planning the death of Seth Warner with his newfound information.

CHAPTER 26

Conner planned his revenge carefully. He decided he would show up at the restaurant at exactly seven fifteen, to make sure Warner and his sister would be seated.

He would identify where he was in the restaurant, and make sure that after he did the deed he was able to escape. Conner didn't care whether or not he got caught. He would not even wear a ski mask or some other disguise. He would pull a Michael Corleone—walk right up, shoot him, make 100 percent sure he was dead, and then exit the restaurant quickly.

At that moment, Conner decided he wanted to say something before he pulled the trigger. Just to make sure that, right before his death, Seth Warner would know why he was being taken out. Conner decided, "This is for Cassie, you son of a bitch," would be a sufficient message for him to deliver to Seth.

Conner walked back and forth through the apartment, pointing the gun at a chair to simulate Seth's murder. He even set up a table with chairs to create a realistic environment, pacing back and forth to make sure he created the exact experience he wanted to. He remembered how much recoil occurred at the shooting range, so he wanted to make sure he compensated for it if he had to shoot him twice or the first bullet missed him. He wanted to leave nothing to chance.

Conner made an inventory of what could go wrong. A bullet had to be in the chamber, so he practiced pulling back the slide incessantly. It was better to have the gun go off by mistake than risk being tackled by another patron or, worse yet, being attacked by Seth himself if the gun failed to fire.

When arriving at the restaurant, he would cock the gun so a bullet was in the chamber, then he could just pull the trigger. No room for mistakes.

Thursday night was like Christmas Eve to Conner. He was finally going to be able to get the revenge he'd been thirsting for. He was fantasizing about the murder of Seth Warner. He could see it—he enters the restaurant, pulls the pistol out of his long wool black coat, and shoots the psychopath in the head and face twice.

As he drifted off to sleep, the images of killing Seth were juxtaposed with his longing for Cassie. The phantom pain attacked him again, where he remembered Cassie wasn't here to comfort him. He imagined that if Cassie were still here, she would enthusiastically help him plan the murder, looking around corners that even he hadn't thought of.

CHAPTER 27

The day came and it was a calming one for Conner. He visited some of his favorite areas in Seattle, making sure to cherish the memories he made with Cassie at each one. He got teary-eyed and welled up at some places that were particularly important to the couple, like Shiki Sushi. He figured if he was going to jail, he might as well soak up these attractions and enjoy them one last time.

When he returned to his apartment, he was all business. He checked, double-checked, triple-checked, and quadruple-checked his Glock 19. He dressed in jeans and a sweater and covered himself with his jet-black wool coat, specifically because the pockets were big enough to hide his firearm.

Conner hailed a cab and got dropped off a few blocks away from the restaurant. He figured that if he was left at the door of the restaurant, it might be easier to connect him with this murder.

As he wandered toward the restaurant, Conner slipped his hand into his pocket and caressed the gun. He wanted to be absolutely sure he had complete control of this dangerous weapon.

The restaurant itself couldn't have been more ideal. It was right on a corner with gigantic windows. The layout would make it easy to find Seth from outside the restaurant. Conner could even shoot him through the glass, but he thought better of it because he wanted to make sure he communicated that he was dying because of what he did to Cassie.

Conner slinked by the entrance and began surveying the restaurant, hands in his pockets. It took him about twelve seconds to find Seth. He was wearing a dark brown sweater and squarish eyeglasses. He was sitting at a table for two, obviously in deep conversation with his sister, who was a good-looking brunette with a round face punctuated by beet-red cheeks. She reached out and brushed Seth's arm playfully and they both began to laugh.

"You won't be laughing for long," Conner said under his breath.

A strange feeling came over Conner. It wasn't nervousness or a rapid heartbeat. It was a funny feeling that left him uneasy. His hands started shaking. He clenched his fists tight to try to stop it, but it just got worse. He shook out his hands. They finally stopped shaking.

"All right, it's time to kill this motherfucker," Conner grumbled. He slid his hand into his pocket to pull out his gun. He slowly pulled the slide back and observed a bullet entering the chamber. He moved toward the restaurant door, ready to pull the handle and swing it open.

Conner began to talk to himself again. *Wait a second. So I kill him? So what? He just dies. He doesn't have to live through the pain that I have now... and will feel for the rest of my natural-born life. And I'm making it as painless as possible by shooting him in the head. He doesn't get to suffer the way Cassie did. What the fuck am I really accomplishing?*

CHAPTER 28

Conner closed his eyes, held his breath, and quickly darted away from the restaurant door. There was a loud *piff* sound. He collided with a short woman with curly reddish hair and a large dark object fell from her hands. As she fell back swiftly, she made no effort to break her fall, reaching instead for the falling object.

Crack. Zeeeeeeng. Waaaaarrroooo. The loud noise emanated from the jet-black violin case as it crashed against the ground. "No," the woman shrieked as the case flung open, revealing the damaged instrument. "Oh my God, no," she whimpered as she crawled toward the instrument case to assess the damage.

Conner shook his hands out and continued to walk down the street, all the while thinking, *Why don't you watch where the fuck you're going, lady?* As he took his seventh step, he froze, thinking of the poor woman he so callously knocked to the ground and the violin he had broken, something that meant a lot to her.

He walked back to where he had left her, cowering over her damaged violin.

She had taken it from the case and had begun to piece it back together with futility.

"Ma'am," Conner uttered timidly. "I'm so sorry. I wasn't watching where I was going. Please..."

"You get the hell away from me." She spat venom as she rose and confronted her offender. "Do you have any idea what you've just done?"

"I'm sorry. It was an accident," Conner sheepishly moaned.

"Accident? Accident? This was my great-grandfather's violin," the woman screeched as she thrust the destroyed instrument at him. "This is an antique. It was made in 1876. It is irreplaceable. It is completely ruined." She began to panic as the tears streamed down her face. Her eyes were becoming dilated. She was shaking, hatred and loss coursing through her veins. Her lower lip began to violently quiver.

"This is a Stradivarius. A Stradivarius! Do you even know the meaning of that word, you fucking idiot? It is a priceless instrument."

"Listen, please calm down," Conner said in a very steady voice. "I can't apologize enough." Conner himself began to get a bit emotional, feeling empathetic for her loss. "My brother owns an instrument repair shop. I promise he can fix it," he said sheepishly.

The woman took a split-second break from her combined anger and anguish and let out a sarcastic laugh. "Are you fucking kidding me, guy? How naïve are you?" As she said this, she switched back to anger. "You can't fix this. It is now worthless, thanks to you. It will *never* sound the same again. It is completely goddamned ruined." Her words came out like flaming bullets intended to strike Conner and make him experience her agonizing pain.

Conner searched for the exact phrase that would calm her down and convince her his brother could work miracles on her now damaged prized possession.

"If it's completely ruined anyway, there is no harm in me taking it to my brother to see what he can do with it." He made sure to avoid putting his statement in the form of a question so she couldn't say no.

"Actually, you're right, you insensitive prick. I might as well throw this in the trash can over there," she said sarcastically. It took everything in her to resist the urge to say, *Now get the fuck away from me and throw yourself in the trash. Asshole.*

"Tell you what," he said, desperately trying to calm her down.

"Give me the violin and your contact information. I'll have my brother repair it, and then I promise I'll get it back to you."

At this point, Conner was not even sure why he was so insistent on taking the slight wooden corpse with him.

The woman rolled her eyes. The tears started to subside and her anger began to fade a bit. "All right, here." She gently placed the cracked violin against the red felt that lined the case. She closed the lid and latched three of the four metal clasps, since the fourth one broke on impact.

The woman rose and handed Conner the violin case, which now included the remnants of her once flawless musical instrument. She shook her head as she drew a white card out of her small magenta clutch and flipped it in Conner's direction. She opened her eyes wide and leaned in toward Conner, as if she expected him to say something.

"Thanks. Again, I'm so sorry, and I'll get this fixed as soon as possible," Conner said in an apologetic tone as he quickly snatched the card out of her hand.

"Fixed? Don't say fixed to me again," she said, once again getting visibly upset. "It is completely destroyed. I assure you there is no way that anyone can fucking fix this."

"I'll see what I can do. My name is Conner Denton, by the way," he said as he clumsily slid the business card into his front pocket and outstretched his right hand, hoping for a handshake that would serve as a show of peace.

"I don't really give a fuck who you are." She shrugged. "In fact, I hope I never see you or that violin ever again. It's just too painful." Her eyes began to well up and her head started to shake.

Conner took that as his cue. As he was about to turn and walk away, he squinted his eyes and said, "Well, what's your name?" not sure why he asked this question. Without missing a beat, the mystery woman wiped the last few tears from her eyes and cleared her throat.

"It's on the card."

Conner bit the inside of his bottom lip, making a face as if he was getting ready to blow into a trombone. Not knowing what to say, he nodded his head, slowly turned to walk in the opposite direction, and left with the black violin case under his left arm, clinking against the gun inside the pocket of his coat.

As he walked away, he left her standing there, glaring at the back of his head. She folded her arms and cocked her head to the side. He pulled the card out of the right-front pocket and tilted it toward the light from a streetlamp.

Julia Farelli. First Chair. Seattle Symphony Orchestra.

CHAPTER 29

"Are you sure you didn't take this thing by the handle and smash it over and over again on the sidewalk?" Joseph said as he grabbed his eyeglasses by the frame and moved them down his nose. "I find it hard to believe that this damage was done by simply dropping it from three feet in the air while it was in a case."

"Very funny, bro," Conner said as he leaned with his back against a beam in the messy warehouse, arms crossed high on his chest. "I'm telling you, it just dropped to the ground after I ran into her, and the case flew open when it hit..."

"You must have run into her pretty hard, then," Joseph said while focusing intently on the broken violin.

Joseph assessed the damage, which was pretty bad. The neck was completely cracked in half, with only two strings connecting it to the body. This was not so troubling to him because the neck was not intrinsic to the sound. What concerned him most was that there was also a large crack on the table of the fragile instrument, from the lower bout to the middle bout, cutting across the f-holes, where the sweet sounds originated when Julia had drawn the rosined bow countless times. This crack went straight through the sound post, sealing the violin's fate. Julia was right; it was impossible to restore, and it would never sound the same again.

The bow itself wasn't fractured, but the hair was a bit frayed, prompting Joseph to nod to himself that he should replace the hair as well, for good measure.

Joseph was in awe of the instrument. Stradivarius violins were extremely rare and expensive. There were just more than two hundred Stradivarius violins left in the world. They were known for legendary craftsmanship and unparalleled sound. He had only seen one in his life, and it was behind glass. He was certainly a fanboy and in utter disbelief that he was touching one.

"Can you fix it?" Conner questioned, unfolding his arms and motioning toward the damaged wooden antique. "Can you fix it?" Conner said again, loudly, after not receiving an answer from his little brother.

"It's pretty bad. Probably the worst I've ever seen," Joseph said as he ran his fingers softly over what was left of this once great instrument. A table lamp illuminated the pile of splintered spruce and maple. "I'll see what I can do."

"All right," Conner shot back. "How long will it take?"

Joseph furrowed his brow, licking his lips as he made a face that made Conner think he didn't know the answer to his question.

"Probably about a month," Joseph finally said after twelve full seconds.

"A month?" Conner squealed in disbelief. "Why so long?" he whined like a spoiled child on a road trip.

"Look," Joseph shouted as he shot Conner the look of death. "I've got to knit the cracks back together seamlessly, with precision accuracy. This is a microscopic operation. I can't just replace the face with another one. That would defeat the whole purpose of the restoration. The broken fragments need to be nurtured and gently eased back into place. Because it's easy for the pieces to slip out of alignment, this needs to be progressively adhered, and I refuse to use patches or studs because that will jeopardize the integrity of the sound. Plus, I'm not going to smooth and re-varnish it because I'm of the belief that the original varnish contributes to the brightness of a violin's sound, and it definitely impacts the item's value. This is a painstaking operation that would take most restorers who specialize in violins eight to twelve months. I'm giving it back to you in one. Be happy."

Conner was stunned. He had no idea what this process entailed. He could see that Joseph was upset. He wished to keep the peace with his brother. He was asking a lot of him.

"OK. OK, baby bro. Do your thing," Conner stated. "Just let me know how much it costs."

"I'm doing this one for free," Joseph said with all seriousness. "You don't even know how much this is going to cost. Plus, if I can pull this one off, it will be my greatest accomplishment. You know this is a Stradivarius, right?"

Conner knew better than to argue with his brother about such things. He nodded his acquiescence and made his way to the table to assess the damage himself once more.

His brother was right. This was an impossible job. The violin was permanently damaged, and Conner himself recognized that it was surprising that such a short drop could cause such extensive damage. Shaking his head over the once magnificent and intrinsically valuable instrument, Conner stared at his brother, mouthing "thank you."

CHAPTER 30

When Conner got back to his apartment, it was raining pretty heavily. He ran and jumped into bed, turning his head toward the foot of the bed and placing his feet up against the cool glass, which was being pelted with large drops of water. He couldn't help but start to cry. He remembered the last time he was in bed with Cassie, watching the curtains flow in the wind. The drops of rain reminded him of her tears, and he couldn't help but recall the savage way in which she was killed. He didn't want to, but he went to a bad place. He imagined the terror as the small blade sliced through her neck, face, and chest. He started to again feel the phantom pains of what he assumed she'd experienced. He tried to put those images out of his mind. But what was left was a deep sense of loss. A loss he knew would never be lessened or extinguished.

"God, I wish I could make him feel this pain," Conner whispered as he lightly kicked the glass, making sure not to crack or shatter the window.

Conner took one last kick at the window, harder this time. He swung his legs around and pulled the covers over his thin body. He stopped sobbing just as his eyes fluttered shut. He perked back up when he saw the black Glock 19 resting on the dresser. He thought of hiding it in case he got any visitors the next day. Instead, his tired state kept him in bed. He needed sleep. He was exhausted. He thought he would fall asleep fast. And after a few more shaky sobs, his eyes closed tight, and he began to enter a subdued state.

Conner's dreams were unusually cruel. He was in a dark cave, and he heard Cassie's voice screaming, *Conner. Help me. Heeeeelp.* Conner was navigating the dark maze without success. Every time he seemed to get close to her, he found those cries were just echoes bouncing off the cave walls. He began to falter and fall as the ground's undulations got more and more treacherous. He finally found a swelling red door and opened it. There he saw Cassie tied to a wooden chair with lacerations throughout her perfectly chiseled body, crying for him. She was wearing a satin nightgown that was stained red and pink with blood, and black smudges that looked like motor oil. Right as Conner lunged forward to grab her, he fell into a large gaping hole. He landed on a rough floor, gun in hand. He saw Seth zip in and out of the light. He pulled the trigger, but the bullets evaded Seth. Conner was powerless; dropping the gun and attacking Seth with his fists, he was still ineffective. Sensing his impotence, Seth grabbed Conner's throat and began to squeeze.

"Jesus Christ," Conner screamed as he awoke and reached for the door, gazing at the area where his lover was stripped of her life. Conner sat up immediately and yelled, "Fuck." He thought to himself that he wanted this torture to stop and asked himself, and God, *When will it ever stop?*

Conner jumped up, grabbed his gun off the dresser, and pushed the release button hard, and the magazine popped out of the bottom. He put the gun in one drawer and the magazine in the other, silently wishing that he would never sleepwalk only to have his subconscious kill himself to erase all this excruciating, indelible pain.

He ambled slowly back to the bed, sat down, and then slammed his head on the pillow. After many more minutes of sobbing and hyperventilating, he finally calmed down and drifted into deep, dreamless sleep.

CHAPTER 31

Conner found that the clouds lifted, and he heard birds tweeting outside as he stirred. He thought it would be a nice day for a walk to the local coffee shop to start planning his revenge, using lessons learned from the botched first attempt.

As Conner wandered toward Caffe Ladro, he inhaled deeply through his nose and squeezed his eyes shut. He always loved the smell of Seattle the day after it rained hard. He even cracked a little half smile as he exhaled, which was a rarity these days.

There was a small line at Caffe Ladro, which annoyed Conner for some reason. He kept on rolling his outstretched hand, whispering, "C'mon, c'mon, c'mon," quietly to the patrons before him.

"Triple espresso," said the short, stocky customer in front of him.

Conner rolled his eyes.

"We can't do triples. We could do a double or a quad," Sandy said from behind the counter.

"Wuh, oh, uh, OK," the spherical-shaped man uttered, not understanding why this was the case.

Conner leaned in. "Look, they only have a duo espresso maker. They can't make a triple." Conner motioned to the espresso maker with the *Seattle Times*.

"Oh, cool. Thanks for the explanation," the man mumbled. "I do appreciate it. Gimme a quad, please."

Conner nodded and grunted. After the man paid for his large order and moved toward the delivery counter, Conner stepped up. "Large latte, extra wet."

"Anything else?" Sandy queried.

"Uh, yeah. Let me get a blueberry scone. And this paper."

"All righty." Sandy smiled. "That will be six forty-seven."

Conner stuffed the *Seattle Times* under his armpit, whipped his credit card out, and tapped it gently, punching a few numbers in and shuffling over to grab his drink.

Sssssssssssssssssshhhhhhhhhhhhhhh. Cccccccccccccchhhhhhhhhhhh. Eeeeeeeeeeeeeeeeeeeehhhhhhhhhhhh. The espresso machine cried out and steamed the milk that would make up the bulk of his large café latte. After a few minutes, they slid the filled cup over toward Conner, and he snatched it up quickly.

Conner swatted the newspaper down on the armrest of an Adirondack chair outside, as if there was a menacing mosquito there. He plopped down and took a sip of his hot latte, enjoying the warm liquid as it funneled down his throat.

As he began the internal dialogue he'd promised himself, he removed a pen from his pocket and pressed his thumb on the top to click it open.

Conner remembered his plea to himself the night before. *I wish I could make him feel this pain.* In the margin of the newspaper, he wrote, "Feel my pain."

Conner's mind began to wander. He resigned himself to the fact that killing Seth wasn't going to be enough. Any way he looked at it, he couldn't justify this in his mind. Sure, if Conner killed him, Seth would likely spend all of eternity roasting in Hell for dispatching the love of Conner's life, and who knows what other atrocities. But what if there wasn't a Heaven or Hell? Certainly, Conner's prayers of bringing Cassie back were not being answered.

He continued to ponder. What if dying was just that, the ending of someone's life? What if killing Seth would just stop his consciousness and there was no afterlife? The way Conner looked at it, death was just letting him off easy.

"Torture." Conner jotted this on the newspaper underneath his goal statement. "Torture, just like the torture I will have to feel throughout the rest of my life."

Conner sighed deeply. "I want to torture him just like the torture I feel." Conner said these words to himself under his breath.

Eureka. Conner had it. He would kill whoever was closest to Seth Warner. That would be the only way for him to make Seth feel the exact same loss, agony, and hopelessness that Conner would endure for the rest of his life.

Conner began to get excited about this prospect. He began to scribble notes on the margins of the *Seattle Times*. He remembered Bob the private eye saying that he was close to his sister. His sister was the woman that Conner saw having dinner with Seth the night he was to kill him. What satisfaction it would be to murder his sister in front of Seth. It would be poetic justice. The perfect dose of revenge.

But what of his sister? What about her thoughts and feelings? Her range of human emotions. She had done nothing wrong. She was completely innocent. Why take her life?

"Fuck it," Conner said. "This is a means to an end. He took an innocent life, now I'm taking an innocent life," he whispered shallowly. "Tit for tat."

Conner justified this further by recalling the gruesome way Seth murdered Cassie, and he figured that he was being humane by simply blowing her brains out. In fact, that was the reason that Conner knew Seth committed the murder. It was the murder weapon. Conner knew specifically that Seth came at Cassie with an X-Acto knife. He remembered her saying that he was an art student and that's how they would mock up artwork at Washington State. This minor detail was the only thing that made Conner proof positive that it was Seth who had carried out the killing of his innocent fiancée.

Conner began to think about this further. *How could Seth possibly be close to any human being? How could he love another and so callously take someone's life in a most gruesome and heartless way? Was it just an act? Is he truly a sociopath who has no empathy and no love in his heart for another human being?*

Conner thought through this for quite a while, ultimately deciding that this plan was sound. The only way to truly get revenge for the horrific act of murdering Cassie would be to kill the person or persons closest to Seth. This would be the only way to transfer the devastation Seth brought to Conner's life back to him.

Conner's eyes began to well up. All these thoughts of Cassie's brutal murder were stirring up deep-rooted emotion in Conner. He bowed his head and wiped a developing tear from his left eye with his shoulder. He took an ample drink of his latte to clear up the lump in his throat. Afterward, he took a deep, chattering breath and exhaled loudly.

Conner sprang out of his chair and started walking as he tore out the sections of newspaper that had his notes on them. He shredded them as best he could by tearing them in smaller and smaller pieces and began to drop them a few shreds at a time into recycle bins as he headed back to his school for the first time in weeks. Better to not leave evidence of his plot, he thought. After a long walk, Conner showed up at his school, which had been filled by a rotating band of substitute teachers since he took leave after the murder. When he arrived, he was met with a gorgeous flower arrangement and a sign that said, "We missed you, Mr. Denton." Conner did his best to hold back the tears; he didn't want to show any weakness to his loyal students. He walked up to the whiteboard and scrawled a few information sources the class had been discussing on his last day before the incident. He paced around the room for a while and slyly uttered, "So, what did I miss?"

CHAPTER 32

"Bob, are you there?" Conner quizzed. "Is that you?"

"Yeah, it's me," Bob answered. "Is this Conner again?"

"Yes, it's me," Conner said excitedly, hands shaking as he pressed his phone against the side of his face. "I have a request."

"What can I help with?" Bob gruffly responded.

"I need more information on Seth Warner. I wasn't able to connect with him during the dinner, so I need to know where he's going to be over the next few weeks."

"Hang on a sec." Bob rolled his chair over to his filing cabinet. After fumbling through his files, he dug out Conner's folder. He rolled back to his desk, slammed the folder on his desk, and licked his fingers.

As he opened the file folder, a large red "Paid" stamp was pressed on the first document.

"Well, I don't think we had any other idea of his whereabouts except for the dinner with... with... her... Wait a minute." Bob coughed.

"What? What is it?" Conner piped up eagerly.

Bob cleared his throat. "He is having a package delivered to his sister's apartment in Bellevue next week. It requires a signature."

"What time? Where exactly?" Conner squealed, his excitement palpable.

"It's supposed to be delivered between 5:00 p.m. and 7:00 p.m. Saturday. I can text you the address and apartment number," Bob offered.

"Cool. You can bill me for this," Conner said, his voice shaking this time.

"Not a chance. We already had this information from the work we already did. I just dug it out for you." Bob chuckled.

"All right. Whatever you say. Just make sure you text me that address," Conner urged, with more intensity this time.

Beedop, Conner's phone buzzed a few minutes later. He tilted the phone away from his head and glanced at a text message with the following address: 10349 NE 10th Street, Apartment 850, Bellevue, WA 98004.

"Awesome. Thanks." Conner placed his thumb on the "END" button and clicked back to the text message. He took a deep breath, pressed on the address, and saw a pin drop on his maps app where the killing of Seth Warner's sister would occur.

CHAPTER 33

"I'm done," Joseph creaked, obviously cracking a sly smile on the other end of the phone.

"Done with what?" Conner assumed that he'd pissed off Joseph for the last time and he was officially disowning him.

"With the Stradivarius," Joseph said. "The violin. I'm done with the restoration."

"Done?" Conner sprang up from laying on his couch. "Are you serious? You told me it would take a month."

Joseph shot back quickly, "It was an amazing restoration. What an opportunity. I mean, to repair a million-dollar violin."

"What the hell are you talking about?" Conner asked, puzzled. "A mi—"

"You really don't know much about musical instruments, do you?" Joseph waited for an answer, but Conner was silently shaking his head on the other line, clearly imperceptible to Joseph. After spending countless days in Joseph's shop, he would have thought some of the knowledge would rub off on Conner. And even if he didn't learn a whole lot, it was common knowledge that Stradivarius violins are world-famous, both for their history and their value.

"A Stradivarius is a valuable piece of history. They were developed by an Italian family in the seventeenth and eighteenth centuries. They supposedly have a unique sound that has never been able to be reproduced," Joseph panted with excitement. "They rarely ever change hands, but they have been known to sell between $400,000 to $4 million or more." Conner gasped. He was incredulous and clearly oblivious to the fact that the violin in question was so expensive. But now the reaction of the redhead made a whole lot more sense.

"I'm actually really surprised that someone was just carrying this around. It really belongs in a museum or behind bulletproof glass somewhere."

"Oh. I just, I had no idea. I mean, she was absolutely irate when I broke it, but I just figured it was worth a few thousand bucks," Conner sheepishly said.

"Well, I got it done," Joseph quipped. "I spent all night the other night knitting this thing back together by hand. You wouldn't even know it was broken."

This was truly the crown jewel of his restoration career, to which he was justifiably proud. He even surprised himself with the intensity and precision in repairing the instrument. As if he were able to channel a sort of divine musical intervention.

"Dude, I can't thank you enough," Conner boomed. "Can I come by tomorrow morning and pick it up?"

"Sure thing, brother." Joseph smiled. "Sure thing."

CHAPTER 34

Conner hung up the phone with Joseph and took a tour around his apartment. He dug through some bills and letters on his desk. He pulled open a few drawers and shuffled some items around.

Finally, he made for his closet and dug through his coat pocket. Sure enough, he was able to locate Julia Farelli's business card.

Conner fished his phone out of his pocket and dialed the mobile phone number on the card. It rang and rang and went to voicemail. Conner hit "END" and dialed the number again. It rang exactly three times, and someone picked up.

"Hello," the woman's voice uttered, unrecognizable to Conner.

"Uh, hey. This is Conner. Um. I met. I'm the one." Conner's head started racing, not knowing exactly what to say. "I. Uh. I have your violin."

After a short pause, the woman's voice came back on the line.

"Fuck off."

The line went dead. Conner gritted his teeth and stared at the phone. He thought it might be better to wait. Maybe call her back in a few days after the pain subsided. He thought better of it, though. If this violin truly had the sentimental and intrinsic value that he thought it did, the pain of its destruction would not subside anytime soon. He knew all about pain and loss. He thought it would be best to just get it over with and try the best he could to get the violin back to her. He had plenty to do in a short period of time, planning a murder and all. Conner hit the call button twice to redial her.

Blooooooooooooom, blooooooooooooom, blooooooooooooom, the phone wailed.

"Can't you take a hint, buddy?"

"Listen to me," Conner yelled. "I have your Stradivarius. My brother repaired it. He spent a lot of time and effort doing this, and I would appreciate the opportunity to give it back to you."

Julia sighed and cleared her throat. Her voice started to crack. "It will never sound the same. I think seeing it again, even repaired, would be too painful. It would have new varnish on it, a new face. It will never be the same agai—"

"No, listen. He didn't re-varnish it. He didn't put on a new face," Conner interrupted.

"That's impossible. I know a few things about violin repair, you know," Julia lectured.

"Just meet me tomorrow. I'll give it back to you and you never have to see me again," Conner said.

There was a long pause. Julia was puzzled about the repair process and was actually curious about how someone was able to repair a smashed violin without replacing the face and re-varnishing the violin.

"What time?" Julia asked, point-blank.

"How about 11:00 a.m.?" Conner responded.

"OK," Julia said. "I'll be at work. Can you meet me in front of Benaroya Hall, where the Seattle Symphony is?"

Conner was surprised she relented so quickly. "Oh, sure, sounds good. I'll be there at eleven. Thanks."

"OK, bye." Julia hung up the phone. She was very skeptical about the repair of her violin. Nevertheless, she was still intrigued and extremely cautiously optimistic about getting her violin back.

CHAPTER 35

Conner arrived at his brother's studio at 10:17 a.m.

"What's up, bro? Let me take a look at it," Conner sang with a smirk on his face.

Joseph looked over at his brother and smiled, noting that this was the first time he'd seen him do anything but scowling, crying, and frowning since Cassie's death.

"All righty, check it out," Joseph shot back as he made a beeline to the black violin case, which Conner recognized from that fateful rainy night.

Conner noticed that the case had been repaired too. All the latches and hinges were in perfect working order.

Joseph placed the case gently on the table and popped open the charcoal-black conveyance.

Clock, clock, the case uttered.

As Joseph opened the case, it creaked a little bit and the lid of the case raised to reveal the priceless antique, which had been restored to its former glory.

Conner's head shot forward. His eyes got bigger. "I can't believe this is the same violin." His head moved even closer to the wooden instrument, with a look of shock and disbelief on his face.

"This is absolutely amazing, brother." Conner gently touched the face of the violin with the tips of his fingers. "I don't know how you do it."

"This is my best work, my friend," Joseph proudly espoused. "I can die happy now. This is my masterpiece. My magnum opus."

Conner slowly closed the lid, not wanting to risk any more damage to the newly renovated violin. He carefully closed the latches, bending down to do so to ensure he didn't leave them loose.

"Thanks again, brother," Conner gratefully said. "Now it's on to get this back into its rightful owner's hands."

Joseph smiled as his brother prepared to leave. "One thing," Joseph yelled out.

Conner looked back as he prepared to exit the studio. "What's that?"

"Could I use the before and after pictures I took?" Joseph was surely proud of his work and wanted to share it with others. "I was thinking about using it on my website and sending it in to the musical instrument repair association as a case study."

"Oh, yeah. No problem. Why not?" Conner thought that was the least he could do for this cost-free repair.

Conner exited the studio, proudly carrying the violin case with a genuine smile on his face, very humbled and grateful for his gifted brother.

CHAPTER 36

Conner stood on the corner of University and 3rd Avenue, whistling as he glanced around, looking for Julia. It was 11:03. He actually didn't remember much about what she looked like. Last time he saw her it was dark and rainy, and she was crying, with bloodshot eyes, and yelling at him at the top of her lungs. All he could remember was that she was a redhead.

"Hello," a voice from behind him delicately said. "I'm Julia."

Conner spun around and made eye contact with the woman. Yes, his memory served him right. She was a redhead with emerald-green eyes and pale skin. Conner noticed that her ears were too big for her round head, and she had a wide nose, but he barely recognized her because she was not yelling and crying. She wasn't attractive by conventional standards, but in this forum she exuded confidence.

Conner froze. He didn't know what to say. He felt like he was in junior high, being speechless in front of a girl at a school dance. Just as he was about to utter a few choice words, Julia piped up.

"I believe you have something for me?" Julia cocked her head and peered down at the violin case that Conner clutched in his arms.

"Yes, here it is." Conner released his viselike grip and extended the case to her. Julia furrowed her brow and put her thin, snowy-white hands under the violin. She brought it over and rested it on the edge of a cement planter and clicked open the violin case.

As she slowly propped open the lid, Conner noticed that a glint of light reflected off of the violin and painted her face with a dark yellowish glow as she took a deep breath. It was almost regal. When she gazed at the renovated Stradivarius, she put her hand over her mouth and tears began coming down her cheeks.

"I... I can't believe it. It looks exactly the same."

Julia slowly lifted the wooden artifact out of the case and examined it. She couldn't believe her eyes. The cracks in the face had been expertly repaired. The back of the violin was immaculate. The neck looked completely perfect. Without looking at the case, she grabbed for the bow, which had a fresh batch of horsehair. She rosined the bow, lifted the violin to her neck, and began to draw the bow across the flawless strings.

As the sound began to emanate from the expertly repaired violin, Conner was struck by how clear it sounded. Julia was obviously a world-class expert in the art of playing the violin, but it sounded particularly perfect. She played an arrangement using every single string and just about every finger position.

Julia was amazed at the sound. Although the violin had an intrinsically rich sound by virtue of it being a Stradivarius, something had changed. For whatever reason, through the restoration, the violin's sound had actually *improved*. The sounds that it delivered were far better than before the repair and even better than the latest-and-greatest violins that were available to modern-day musicians. The violin sounded better than it ever had before, and better than any other violin Julia had ever heard in her life.

Julia began to weep. She placed the bow back in the case and lowered the violin so it was resting on her knees. She was so amazed and overwhelmed that the violin produced a magical, almost heavenly sound, far better than it sounded before, that she began to sob, wiping her eyes vigorously so they didn't drip down on the magnificent instrument.

"That's my cue," Conner whispered as he shuffled away from her slowly, and then turned to walk away. He made it about forty feet away before Julia called out to him.

"Hey," Julia's voice boomed. "Wait a sec."

Julia quickly placed the violin in the case and repositioned the bow. She clicked the latches shut firmly and grabbed the case, walking swiftly toward Conner.

Conner saw this and began to walk even faster.

"Come here, please." Julia began to stop crying, but she started to panic as she pursued Conner.

Conner paused and decided to turn back. Julia jogged toward him and got within five feet of him.

"Thank you. Thank you so much. I can't believe this. It's so amazing." Julia was trembling, and she began to sob once again.

Conner looked around, noticing that they were making a scene. "No problem. It was all my brother. He did an exceptional jo—"

"Let me make it up to you," Julia proclaimed. "Can I pay you? Let me take you to dinner."

"No thanks. The fact that you are so happy is good enough for me." Conner began to turn and jog away again.

"No, please. Don't walk away. Let me take you to dinner. Wherever you want. You'll never know how much this means to me." Julia began to calm down but was still visibly shaken.

"I'm OK. Don't worry about it." Conner began to walk faster as Julia pursued him.

Julia grabbed his elbow and swung him around. "I insist. I have to pay you back. You don't understand."

"Look, lady. I barely got you here. You have called me just about every dirty word imaginable. I got your violin. Be happy. Now leave me alone." Conner was now getting angry as he stood there in front of her.

"You don't understand." Julia began crying again. "This violin has never sounded this good before. This is nothing short of a miracle. I must pay you back."

Conner thought for a bit. Was it a good idea to go to dinner with this person? No. Was Conner singular in his focus to find and kill Seth's sister? Yes. Was Julia contributing to this goal? Absolutely not.

Conner's eyes fell. He also realized one thing. He was lonely. In addition to the painful suffering he was going through and the deep sense of loss he felt every single day, the idea of dinner out with a woman actually appealed to him. Maybe this could get his mind off of the loss of Cassie. Maybe this would make him feel normal, if only for a brief period of time. Maybe he could forget, if only for a fleeting moment.

"Um... All right. I'll go," Conner muttered begrudgingly.

"OK. Good." Julia's face began to perk up. "Will tonight work? You name the place and time. I can meet you there."

Conner thought for a moment, which felt like a year to him. "Let's do Le Coin. Will that work?"

Julia pressed her lips together and shook her head vigorously. "Yes. Yes, that works perfectly. Seven o'clock tonight? Sound good?"

Conner nodded his head slowly. "Yep. Works for me."

Julia stood there as Conner began to walk briskly away from her. She wrapped her arms around her violin case even more tightly, hugging it as she began to cry again, and made her way back into the building.

CHAPTER 37

Conner arrived at Le Coin at 6:55. Julia was already there. As he cautiously entered the restaurant, the hostess greeted him and he looked around, seeing Julia waving at him. "I'm meeting someone here," Conner said loudly as he motioned to Julia. The hostess waved him back with a smile, and he began to make his way to the table.

Julia was wearing a little black dress with a large green necklace that matched her eyes perfectly, which Conner failed to notice. Conner was in black slacks and a blue button-down shirt. He pinched the back of the chair and slid it out so he could sit down.

Julia piped up. "Thanks again for meeting me. This is the least I can do for all that you've done for me."

"Like what?" Conner said flippantly. "I was the one who broke your violin, remember? It was just fortunate that my brother happens to be a gifted violin repairman."

"I see." Julia's face sank. "Maybe I should have invited him to dinner."

Conner wrapped his hand around his neck and pulled it around to his throat, feeling his coarse, stubbly neck. "Sorry. I do appreciate this. I'm glad he was able to fix it."

"Fix it?" Julia shouted. "It plays better than it ever has. What your brother did was nothing short of magical."

"Yeah, I guess he went overboard. At first he said it was going to take at least a month, and he got it done in a couple of weeks. I think he just got into a zone and became almost obsessed with it." Conner began to loosen up and sink into his chair.

"I can't believe that. It usually takes much, much longer for a repair of this kind. I can't explain it. He must be extremely talented." Julia's voice began to get louder to drown out the background noise in the restaurant.

"Extremely talented. Yeah, I can't believe it either. You would think that a repair or renovation would denigrate the sound, not make it better." Conner began to look puzzled.

"That's exactly what happens usually. And the fact that he didn't replace the face or re-varnish it," Julia pondered. "It's unbelievable. Even more," Julia continued, "I absolutely wanted to kill you that night. Right now, all I want to do is kiss you."

Conner rubbed his head and cracked a half-grimaced, uncomfortable smile.

The couple ordered a bottle of Cabernet Sauvignon from the Willamette Valley region of Oregon. They talked about food and wine and where they grew up. Conner learned about the life of a professional violin player. Conner talked about his work as a schoolteacher. They discovered that they were both foodies. That they both loved to travel, particularly internationally.

Julia began to trace the rim of her wine glass with her petite fingers. "So, tell me more about you. What are some of your dreams?"

Conner took a deep breath, thinking about this question differently. Before Cassie's death, he had many dreams and goals. Now he was singularly focused on one thing: revenge. He obviously couldn't divulge this, and even if he did, it would have killed the evening. But he felt empty when thinking about his dreams. He couldn't put his finger on one. Not even one. All he felt now was sorrow. With no hope for the future, all of his dreams were now dead.

"To tell you the truth, I don't have many dreams. I know this probably sounds weird, but I'm really a day-to-day guy. I... I used to date this girl, and we would do a lot of that together, but she's, uh. She's, uh, gone."

Julia perked up. "Oh my God, I'm sorry. How long has it been?"

"Several months." Conner began to tear up, not wanting to even think about Cassie being gone.

"Oh, dear, I'm so sorry. That's just awful." Julia shot Conner a genuine look of care and concern.

"Yeah, sorry to be a buzzkill," Conner said. "It's just been consuming my every thought as of late."

"Well, I'm really sorry about that. I know this pales in comparison, but when I went through my divorce, I was in a funk for over a year." Julia tried to console Conner with this statement.

"Oh, yeah, when was that?" Conner queried.

"Oh, a little over a year ago," Julia innocently said.

"Haha." Conner chuckled and cracked a rare smile. "Thanks for trying to cheer me up."

"You got it," Julia said without missing a beat. "We all go through a shitstorm sometimes."

"Yeah," Conner replied as he glared at his wine glass. "We certainly do."

CHAPTER 38

"Conner? You OK?" Julia beckoned. Conner continued to stare at the half-empty wine glass, thinking this was not such a good idea. He wondered why he'd even brought it up, re-opening even a glimpse of this deep, desolate wound. What did he have to gain? Why was he bumming this girl out?

"Yup, I'm fine," Conner snapped. "The nerve is still raw."

"Well, let's change the subject, shall we?" Julia sensed the great loss he was feeling and wanted to alleviate it. "What kind of dessert do you like? Fruity or chocolatey?"

"I'm all about the chocolate," Conner said with a half smile.

"OK, the Chocolate Pot de Crème it is," Julia decided.

The couple enjoyed their dessert and coffee silently, enjoying the decadent confection. After Julia paid the tab, Conner stood up slowly and began to exit the restaurant. Julia followed, almost acting as his shadow as he stepped out onto Fremont Ave.

"Taxi," Conner yelled at the top of his lungs. He yelled the same phrase three more times and shot his arm up into the air before a green taxicab pulled over next to him and skidded to a stop.

Conner made his way over to the rear passenger door, swung it open, and motioned with the other hand for her to get in. *How great was it,* Julia thought, *for Conner to hail a cab for me first? What a gentleman.* Julia strutted toward the cab, grabbed both of Conner's shoulders, and gave him a soft kiss. Conner resisted for a second, but then just let it happen. He took a long breath and bit her lips softly as she touched her tongue to his, squeezing her eyes tightly shut. After a few seconds, she removed her hands from his shoulders, plopped down in the seat of the taxicab, and gazed back at him.

"Thanks for dinner, Conner," she said seductively.

"Thank you," Conner said with his eyes still closed. "Thank you."

CHAPTER 39

As Conner rode home, he reminisced about the kiss. He wondered why she was so forward. Was it because of his confession of his breakup, which was half of a lie? Was she trying to cheer him up? He couldn't figure it out. And Conner kept on thinking what a bad idea it was to get mixed up with a girl right now. He was likely to go to prison for the rest of his life, and that's *if* he got caught. The beauty of Conner's plan involved killing an innocent victim, a total stranger with a black-market gun, so linking him to the crime would be difficult if he was able to make it away from the scene of the crime without detection.

The brakes of the cab squeaked as it stopped at Conner's apartment. Conner gave the cab driver a ten-dollar tip and the driver was visibly grateful. As Conner made his way up the stairs, he started to sway from side to side, now noticing how buzzed he was from the half bottle of wine he enjoyed at the restaurant.

After he shut the door and cranked the lock clockwise, Conner strolled over to the kitchen and pulled open the junk drawer, sliding the Glock 19 out of the drawer and holding it in both hands, caressing it like a delicate flower. He admired how beautiful it was and expressed gratitude to this piece of steel and polymer, which would facilitate the vengeful murder he was about to commit.

Conner started to worry about the gun. What if it didn't fire? What if it jammed? What if the magazine fell out? He'd bought it off of a street hustler, and he had no assurances that it was going to work as planned. Growing more and more concerned, Conner decided to write a checklist of activities he had to perform just prior to the killing. He also became methodical about practicing with the gun. He practiced cocking the gun, aiming it, and reloading. He pushed on the release, slid out the magazine, pulled back the slide, and looked through it to make sure there weren't any bullets in the chamber. After closing the slide with a loud click, he pulled the gun up, aimed it at a brick wall, and dry fired it with a softer click.

As the gun clicked, Conner grinned, looking forward to the day that he could permanently take something away from Seth that he would never get back. He got chills running up and down his spine at the mere thought that he could transfer the agonizing pain and loss from Conner's psyche to Seth's by taking out the person that he held most dear.

Conner picked up the magazine, slid it into the gun with another loud click, placed it down inside the junk drawer, and moved toward the bedroom. He emptied his pockets onto the nightstand, sat down, and took his shoes off. He picked up his shoes, dropped them in the closet, stripped down to his underwear, and walked over to the bed.

Two minutes after laying his head on his pillow, his phone beeped. *Bedope*, the phone cried out.

Conner shuffled his hand around the nightstand, picking up his phone and hitting the home button to see who had texted him.

It was Julia. "Can you talk now?"

Conner abandoned the phone and changed positions, shuffling the sheets with his back to the phone. He was asleep in less than five minutes.

CHAPTER 40

Conner arose to a headache. He grabbed a glass of water from the nightstand, chugging it in hopes that he was just dehydrated and the cool, clear water would cure his pounding headache.

"God," Conner groaned. "I didn't drink *that* much last night." Conner knew that this headache couldn't have been caused by a hangover due to the small amount of booze he'd ingested the night before. It had to be something else.

Conner rolled out of bed, drinking glass in hand, to get more water and some Tylenol. He pushed the glass into the middle of his refrigerator's water dispenser and filled up the glass halfway, bringing it immediately to his lips and taking several slow, labored swigs.

Conner opened up the cupboard above his stove and grabbed a bottle of Tylenol and a bottle of Advil. He spilled two Tylenol pills and three Advil tablets into his hand and popped all five in his mouth and chugged some water to make sure they all went down, thinking that he was covering his bases by swallowing both acetaminophen and ibuprofen.

Conner rubbed his eyes with his fists and walked back over to his bedroom and fell back into his blanket and sheets, pulling them over his head after placing the near-empty glass of water on his nightstand.

After a few minutes of trying to reorient himself, Conner peered over to his phone, noticing that he had two text messages now. Conner clumsily proceeded to the nightstand, almost knocking the glass off, and snatched his phone, swiping to view his texts.

"Can you talk now?" "I really want to see you again." Both were from Julia.

"FUCK," Conner screeched at the top of his lungs, tossing the phone back toward the nightstand, which bounced off and fell facedown on the floor.

Conner rolled over on his back and placed his forearm across his closed eyes, digging it into his face like it was a hacksaw.

"This is all I need," Conner whispered to himself. "All I fucking need."

His initial hesitations were confirmed; Conner did not need anything to distract him from his ultimate goal, and he certainly didn't want to get wrapped up into a relationship where there may be feelings that develop or emotional complications that remind him of the loss of Cassie.

Conner continued to think about it. While he didn't want to get mixed up with this woman, he hadn't been with anyone since Cassie, which was now more than four months ago. He hadn't even desired sex since her death... that is, until last night.

When Julia grabbed him and unceremoniously planted a kiss on his quivering lips, he felt something. For the first time in many months, he felt something. And it was something other than mourning, other than grief, other than that grating, emotional pain that plagued him for just about ev-

JARED BODNAR

ery waking hour since Cassie's grisly murder. A gush of hot blood lit up his heart, which started pounding aggressively. His eyes dilated. His cheeks became flushed. Endorphins coursed through his veins. And it felt good.

Conner reasoned that if he could keep this arrangement physical and make an explicit agreement with Julia that this would not turn into a relationship, it might be a good way to provide some fleeting joy in his life and give him some brief pleasure before going into hiding or jail. After all, if she hadn't been with anyone since her divorce, which she'd alluded to, it might just be a win-win partnership.

Conner fell out of bed, dropped to the floor, and crawled to his phone, sighing happily after flipping it over and noticing that the screen wasn't cracked from his flippant toss. While still on the floor, Conner began tapping on the glass: "I don't think..."

CHAPTER 41

Julia's green eyes glanced down at her purse after her phone beeped. As she fished it out of her bag, she wondered if it was Conner responding back to her. As she pulled the phone out, she grinned and saw that it was Conner.

Her grin soured a bit, though, as she read his response.

"I don't think it's a good idea for me to get into a relationship at this time."

Julia, not discouraged by this, started furiously tapping on her screen.

"Who said anything about that? I just had a good time last nt & want to hang out again."

The text went unread. Conner grabbed a pan out of the cupboard, slid it onto the stove, and turned on the gas. He grabbed some eggs and English muffins out of the refrigerator to whip up a makeshift Egg McMuffin. He slammed down the ingredients and thought to himself about how Cassie would make him food. She would whip up gourmet omelets with shitake mushrooms and spinach. One morning, she even grabbed some filet mignon from a doggie bag and sliced it up to incorporate into a breakfast dish. He applied his front teeth to his lip. He could taste it. He could see her in the kitchen flipping the skillet effortlessly and chopping various ingredients on the bamboo cutting board. He exhaled deeply, almost impossibly deeply.

"Holy fucking shit." Conner breathed in as if he was suffocating and needed air desperately. He couldn't believe what had just happened.

Conner had just had a positive thought about Cassie that didn't end with vivid thoughts and visualizations of her death. It was a good memory. A thought about her that didn't bring back memories of her brutal slaying. Her suffering. Her agonizing death at the hands of a callous coward.

"This is unbelievable," Conner muttered under his breath. "Un-fucking-believable."

Conner backed away from the counter and then slowly returned to make his breakfast. He cracked the eggs very slowly and gently into the greased frying pan. He clumsily shoved the English muffins into the toaster and twisted the knob to the right, causing it to rapidly tick.

Conner made his way back over to the refrigerator, pulling it open and searching the drawers for some cheese, but finding none. He looked for any additional items he could use, thinking again of what Cassie would add to this particular dish. Red onions, nope. Avocado, nope. Peppers, nope. Clearly Conner wasn't the prolific shopper Cassie had been, especially given his recent funk.

Conner flipped the pan, almost dropping the eggs right on the floor. After shaking them around and adjusting them to be in the middle of the pan, he returned them to the burner. The English muffins were just about done, so he retrieved them from the toaster and placed them on a small blue plate.

Conner nodded his head at the pan, grabbed it by the handle, and slid the eggs onto one slice of the English muffin and topped it with the other slice.

Sitting down at his table, Conner stared at his creation and began to think about the object of his revenge. Seth Warner. The man whose sister he would be killing very soon. *What a coward*, Conner thought. *What a weak, disgusting coward.* The hatred returned to Conner's mind and flooded his chest with rage. His throat began to get dry, his eyes started to water, his hands began to shake.

"Nothing will prevent me from achieving my goal," Conner said to himself. "Nothing."

He stared down at his sandwich, not feeling hungry at the moment. He rested his elbows on the table next to the cobalt-blue plate and placed his forehead into his hands, trying to calm himself down so his appetite returned. His headache began to return. He grabbed the English muffin sandwich with both hands and took a small bite.

CHAPTER 42

A cool breeze wafted into the apartment through a cracked window, sending the sheer curtain flying. Conner made his way over to the sink, rinsing off the plate and jamming it into the dishwasher.

He grabbed his phone and sat back down at the table to finish the rest of his lukewarm coffee. He pulled his phone up to eye level and squinted at Julia's text.

"Who said anything about that? I just had a good time last nt & want to hang out again."

Conner noticed another, more recent text: "We can even meet close to your house, so you can walk home."

Conner pondered this text. He knew that this was an unnecessary distraction, but the last kiss that they shared felt... good. It was the first kiss he'd experienced since kissing Cassie goodbye on her way to work that fateful day, which he had since recounted in painstaking detail numerous times.

And what's more, he had finally experienced a positive memory of Cassie, one that was not followed by crippling memories of her death. Whether or not this occurrence was inextricably linked to the encounter with Julia was irrelevant. Perhaps, Conner thought, he was now finally starting to heal.

Conner thought better of it. He knew that this pain would never go away. The person that was his perfect match, his counterpart, his soul mate, was gone forever. This pain created a deep chasm within Conner. One that wouldn't go away no matter what. It would never go away. Again, he wanted Seth to feel this same pain. He wanted him to go through life reliving this pain. This torture. This grief. This loss.

Looking down at the new text, Conner began pressing on the glass with his middle finger. "Do you know where Taylor Shellfish Oyster Bar is?"

Conner stared at his phone for a while, then he blinked a couple of times, placed it gently on the table facedown and picked up his coffee mug and downed it like a shot of Patrón.

He kicked the chair out from underneath him as he rose and moved over to the sink, opening the faucet to rinse out the coffee mug and then placing it clumsily on the dishwasher's top rack.

Wanting to feel the cool metal of the gun again, Conner fished it out of the junk drawer. He raised the gun to his face and inhaled sharply at the site of the bullet ejection point, smelling a faint twinge of gunpowder from multiple shells being thrown violently from the jet-black gun at the gun range. He pointed the gun toward the window, lining up the sight. He then brought the gun toward his chest and pointed it at the wall of the kitchen. Conner then brought the gun around to his lower back, sandwiching it between his pants and his skin. He liked the feel of it. The cold, black, rough feel of it invigorated him. He couldn't wait to point it at Seth's loved one and see the sheer terror in his face.

Bedope. Conner twisted his neck back and glared at his phone, which was still resting facedown on the kitchen table. He grabbed the gun out of his waistline and pointed it at the phone, walking slowly like a cop trying to clear an area. He slammed the gun down next to the phone, picked it up, and peered at the glass screen.

"I can look it up. How does tom at 7 work?"

CHAPTER 43

"Gannet here," the old man gruffly shouted as he picked up the phone.

"Hey, Bob, it's, uh, uh, Conner." Conner's voice was cracking; he was really nervous.

"Hey, kid. How you doing? What do you need?"

"The sister's name. I need the sister's name. What's Seth's sister's name?" Conner's heart started to beat rapidly, and his hand started to shake.

"The sister, the sister, the sister," Gannet repeated. "Hang on a sec."

Conner heard several noises. Filing cabinets opening and closing, papers shuffling, what sounded like a notebook hitting the ground.

After what seemed like twenty minutes, Gannet returned to the phone. "Hey, kid, are you there?"

"Yeah," Conner urgently screamed. "I'm here."

"It's Sarah." Gannet coughed. "Sarah J. Warner."

Conner's back hit the wall and he slid down slowly. "OK, Bob, thanks. That's all I needed, thanks." He then pressed "END" on the phone.

As his butt hit the ground, sliding down the wall, he felt relieved. Relieved that now he knew who he had to kill. He knew her by name. He also knew that he didn't already know her, so he would have no problem taking her innocent life, just so Seth could suffer for the rest of his life and recollect the painful details of her death for his entire existence on this earth. Conner even remembered what she looked like. Brunette with light skin, a round face, and dark-red cheeks.

Conner closed his eyes and began to calm down. His heart rate slowly returned to normal, his tremors subsided, and he started breathing normally again. Conner used his left knuckle to lift himself up and headed over to the bedroom, looking back at his phone along the way. "I can look it up. How does tom at 7 work?"

He looked up from the phone and pondered this development. He asked himself again whether or not this was a good idea. He remembered how close he had grown to Cassie, how she owned his heart, and how devastating her death was to him, being that he had such a strong, deep, meaningful emotional connection to her. Was it really a good idea to start spending time with another woman, especially given what he was about to do?

Conner maneuvered his thumb to the top of the glass and started typing. "Sounds good. See you there," he sent.

As he gently guided the phone into his front right pocket, Conner's mind began to spin. With his constant thoughts, nightmares, and sympathy pains from Cassie's death, his mental and logistical planning for the murder of Sarah Warner, and his preparation to spend the rest of his life in prison or on the lam, there were so many complex emotions and so much tumultuous uproar inside his mind, inside his body, inside his soul.

He was looking for something to intervene. He wanted some semblance of normalcy. He wanted the terror, the homicidal voices, the hatred in his head, to cease. Conner was looking for something to make the pain go away. Something to calm the psychotic commotion in his head. A magic pill, perhaps. Maybe alcohol. Maybe the only solution was a bullet in his own head.

Conner clumsily pulled his phone out of his pocket, staring at the message he just sent. "Sounds good. See you there."

"What the fuck am I doing?" Conner said as he tossed the phone on his bed and walked out of the room.

CHAPTER 44

It was pissing rain when Conner set out for Taylor Shellfish Oyster Bar, right around the corner from his house. With umbrella in hand, he paced toward the restaurant rapidly. When he arrived, he aggressively shook the umbrella and retracted it, and whipped off his coat to shake some additional water off. He glanced around the place, which was light and bright compared to the dark, sopping environment outside. There was a bar in the middle of the restaurant, which was nearly filled up completely. His eyes darted around the room to see if he could spot Julia. Conner placed his hand on the hostess stand.

"I'm meeting someone here. My name's Conner. Is she here yet? Her name is Julia," Conner said.

"I don't think she's arrived yet, but let me check," the hostess, named Sasha, gleefully mentioned as she drew her finger across the table layout floorplan on the hostess podium. "No, doesn't look like it. Table for two?"

"Yes, please," Conner said as he followed Sasha to the two-top table.

Conner glanced at his watch and saw that it was 6:58, so he was a couple minutes early, clearly from his aggressively brisk walking due to the rain.

Seven minutes passed and Conner began to get restless. He was going to wait until Julia arrived to order a drink, but he went ahead and ordered an Elysian Immortal IPA and patiently waited for it to come.

Julia stormed through the door six minutes later. She bobbed her head around, located Conner, and waved quickly to the hostess as she charged toward Conner's table.

"Sorry I'm late," she sang. "Traffic got messed up because of the storm," she said apologetically.

"It's all good," Conner said, squinting at his wristwatch. "I think you're only like five minutes late."

Right on cue, a server named Tony approached the table, as if it was meticulously orchestrated. "Can I offer you some—"

"Do you have a Riesling?" Julia interrupted. "I'll have a glass of Riesling, thanks."

"Of course," Tony said. "I'll be right back with that."

"Grab us a dozen oysters too, please," Conner asked.

"Of course," Tony nobly answered. "Which ones would you like?"

Conner pondered for a few seconds and scanned the menu. "Let's do half Olympia and half Pacific."

"Perfect," Tony agreed. "Great choices."

"Thanks," Conner uttered as his head twisted, following Tony with his eyes back to the kitchen.

"So, thanks for meeting me," Julia said sheepishly. "I know you have concerns, and I totally get it. Just know that I'm not looking to get into a relationship. Truth be told, I have plenty going on with the symphony and my other extracurriculars."

Conner was perplexed. He immediately searched for ulterior motives. Maybe she was trying to get him to put his guard down... to disarm him.

"All right. I appreciate that," Conner said. "I didn't mean to push back on you so hard. I'm just a little... ah, broken up about all this, and I'm experiencing a lot of emotions right now. Don't want to jump in to..." Conner's voice trailed off and he sat there staring at the table.

"It's fine," Julia responded quickly. "I totally understand. I'm not quite over my marriage ending. I'm holding on to a lot of things."

Conner's head shook silently, and he looked into her eyes for the first time at the dinner, not at the table.

"Anyway, let's have a nice dinner. Do you come here a lot?" Julia was trying to point the conversation away from their dreary situations and back to their tasty drinks and great food.

"Uh, yeah. I live just around the corner," Conner said. "Best oysters in Seattle."

"Oh, great. I love shellfish," Julia said energetically. She flipped the napkin off the table and onto her lap.

"Uh, how is the violin?" Conner sensed her desire to change the subject and obliged.

"Plays better than ever," Julia said with a straight face. "I don't know how or what your brother did, but it sounds un-like any violin I've ever heard. Perfect pitch and tone. Much too much body for such a small instrument, which is actu-ally a good thing. He deserves a medal." Julia continued. "I almost don't want to know how he did it. It's like magic. The luster falls off when you know how a trick or illusion is done."

"Yeah, he is amazing. Such a craftsman. He always talks about it as a dying art because everything is going electronic and the musical instrument industry has become commod-itized and the value is lowered. Essentially, costs are so low that instruments are thrown away and replaced if they break or need repairs. They aren't restored."

"Not a Stradivarius," Julia pointed out. "Those have so much value that you have to at least try to repair them. It's just that that night it looked like it was so annihilated that it couldn't have conceivably been repaired."

"So why were you carrying such a priceless item through the streets that night?" Conner queried.

"That's a great question." Julia's voice started to creak. Her eyes started to water. "I've never found a violin that could play like that, so I use it for performances. Believe it or not, I was holding it close to me, with white knuckles. Clutching it as hard as I could, like I always do when I bring it out in public. That's why it was such a shock when it flew out of my grip when I bumped into you."

"Um, you mean I slammed into you," Conner replied. "Walking really, really fast at that. Almost running."

The twelve oysters arrived at the table, which silenced Conner and Julia. Conner sensed this was a great time to divert attention away from the painful memory of the violin fracturing and back to the delightful food.

"So, the Pacific oysters are from the Puget Sound," Conner instructed as he grabbed the lemon and squirted it on top of the entire dish with several swirling motions. "The, uh, Olympia oysters are from Shelton, Washington."

"Sounds great," Julia said as she pinched one of the oysters by its shell and placed it on her plate. Conner began to clumsily spoon out horseradish, mignonette, and cocktail sauce on one of the Olympia oysters and he threw it into his mouth, enjoying the briny flavors as he swished it around and swallowed it down.

Julia began to enjoy hers as well. She considered asking Conner something. Something that had been bothering her since when she first started to get to know him. She decided to put it out there.

"Conner?" Julia asked in a serious tone. "I know you're dealing with a breakup, which is totally understandable, but... is there anything else going on with you?"

Conner scrunched his forehead, surprised by this question. Not wanting to delve down into what was really bothering him, Conner quickly decided to brush her off.

"Not that I know of," Conner casually said, then cleared his throat. "Why do you ask?"

"I don't know," Julia admitted. "It's just..."

Julia leaned back in her chair and exhaled slowly. "It's just that you seem so, so hollow. Like empty, if that makes sense."

Conner began to nod his head and looked down sadly at his plate.

"And I'm sorry, it doesn't seem like a breakup, divorce, or any relationship problems are causing it. When I look at you, I see someone who is vacant. Someone with something weighing him down. I can't even think of the word."

Julia looked up and around the restaurant and back down at the empty oyster shells. She again looked at Conner right in the eyes, and he looked back up at her.

"This may just be how it occurs to me," Julia admitted. "But when I look at you, I see someone who is... damaged."

CHAPTER 45

As the second plate of oysters showed up, this time Virginica and Kusshi, Conner went to reassure Julia, not wanting to get into the gory details of his loss and what had caused him to become a shell of the man he once was.

"You're very perceptive," Conner began. "But it really is just a breakup. Let's just say that we were very, very close and it was a huge shock when she left me." Julia looked him over, sensing that he was just glossing over something else. "OK," Julia apologized. "Maybe my intuition is just off."

But it's 100 percent right on, Conner thought. She knew exactly what was happening. He was masking the pain he was really feeling with a smokescreen cover story. He felt like telling her the whole story. That the love of his life, a love he would never experience for the rest of his life, was gone. And he was plotting revenge on the perpetrator by killing one of his family members to atone for his cowardly act. But he thought better of it. What could that possibly accomplish? Would it help her understand what he was going through?

Would it engender more sympathy? Would it bring Cassie back? Absolutely not.

"So, what happened with your marriage?" Conner asked apologetically. "You said you were in a funk, but you look like you're doing great."

Julia responded immediately. "Well, I'm apparently better at hiding it than you," she winked. "My ex-husband had an affair with someone else in the symphony. They're together now, and I have to work with her almost every single day." Tears welled up in her eyes, but she shook her head slowly and blinked them away. "It's been really hard, but it gets a little better every single day."

"I wish I was there," Conner said. "It seems to get worse and worse every day. They say time heals all wounds, but I don't see that. The only time it ever subsides..." Conner cut himself off, quickly moving the attention back to the food. "So, anyway, the Kusshi oysters are from Vancouver Island, BC, and the Virginica ones are from here in Washington." Conner took another swig of his beer and attempted to improve his mood by enjoying the taste of the salty oysters. Julia prepped and downed another oyster and cracked a smile as it hit her tongue.

"This sounds weird, but the way I've found to best way to handle the depression is by keeping yourself busy, keeping your mind occupied, essentially making yourself distracted," Julia expressed with sympathy. "Do you have any hobbies?"

"Uh, yeah, I have a hobby," Conner jumped in.

It's called planning to kill someone, he thought.

Thinking better of it, he quickly thought of a lie. "Ah, my brother. He's um, teaching me how to repair instruments." He said this almost as if he were asking a question.

"Really?" Julia leapt. "I think that's great. What an amazing way to pass the time."

Beginning to further construct the lie, Conner added to the fabrication. "Yeah, it's strange, though. He is really advanced, as you can imagine, so teaching me is very remedial for him. I'm doing mostly hand-sanding at this point." Conner remembered watching his brother do this on many occasions, so he felt this was a safe bet.

"I'm really glad you're doing that," Julia mentioned. "I assure you that it may not seem like it now, but this will help ease the pain down the road."

"OK, thanks," Conner said. "I sure hope so."

The couple enjoyed the rest of the meal and a few extra adult beverages. The check came, and Julia insisted on paying, being that she was the one who did the inviting. Conner argued for a few seconds but realized he was making a scene and decided to acquiesce.

He followed her out of the restaurant, and as they grabbed their coats and umbrellas, Conner turned to Julia.

"Do you want me to hail you a cab?" Conner said flatly.

Julia shot him back a coy look. "Why don't we go to your place for coffee? You said it was right around the corner." She started to look around the neighborhood.

Conner thought better of it. This was not a good idea. The question did shoot a pang of dopamine through his veins. He actually started to smile, though he fought off this showing of emotion as best he could.

"Sure, why not?" Conner uttered almost involuntarily. He couldn't believe he spoke those words, and scolded himself internally for this mistake.

"C'mon," he motioned. "It's right this way."

Julia smiled somberly, her emerald-green eyes lighting up in the process. She picked her head up and followed the tall, hollow man down the slick sidewalk.

CHAPTER 46

Conner slid the key into the lock and twisted it hard, causing it to make a loud swiveling then clicking sound. He placed his hand on the heavy door and used his left shoulder to force it open.

"Come on in and make yourself at home," Conner awkwardly said as he made his way over to the coffee maker. Julia glanced around with a subdued smile as she hung her dark brown coat on the coat rack.

"I like your place," Julia said. "You must get a ton of sun during the day with all these windows."

"Yeah, thanks. We—I mean—I love that aspect of this place," Conner mumbled as he fiddled around with the coffee filter.

"So where do you live?" Conner blurted out, deciding this time to enunciate every single word instead of mumbling.

"I'm over by Clyde Hill." Julia smiled, and she looked over a few pieces of mixed media art. "It's actually a straight shot to the symphony, believe it or not." Julia motioned toward the sound system. "Do you mind if I put some music on?"

"Uh, yeah, sure. Go ahead. If you can figure that thing out," Conner said in a playful manner. "You're not going to put on classical music, are you?" "Haha," Julia laughed. "Of course not. I have to listen to that for hours on end every day." Julia began fooling around with the knobs and buttons on the sounds system.

Bleeeouuuuuu. Bleeeeeeooooooooo, the stereo blurted at an uncharacteristically loud noise level.

"Whoops, sorry," Julia said as she twisted the volume knob down quite a bit, making it much more pleasant. The stereo played a nice, smooth jazz song, definitely not classical music.

Conner began to relax. He finished grinding the beans and tapped the side of the coffee grinder to get the grounds into the coffee filter. He filled the glass coffee pot half-full with filtered water and slowly poured it into the black coffee maker and pressed the start button.

The coffee maker began bubbling and emitting hissing noises as it dribbled scalding-hot coffee into the coffee pot. Conner joined Julia near the stereo as the coffee brewed.

"Thanks for the music selection. I'm surprised you were able to get this thing to work," Conner said with a scratchy voice and immediately coughed loudly to clear his throat, covering his mouth with both hands.

"I am a musician, you know," Julia joked. "Just kidding. I have the same exact system." She smiled. "I just didn't know it would be turned up full blast."

Conner smiled back, not wanting to admit that he turned it up so high to drown the pain, emotions, and commotion in his head. "Yeah, I like to rock out sometimes." Conner managed to crack an ear-to-ear smile at this point, something that had been very uncharacteristic for him these days. "Looks like the coffee's almost ready," Conner said as he darted toward the coffee maker. Julia followed closely behind.

As Conner gripped the coffee pot, Julia came up behind him and grabbed his hand, pulling it gently around his hip so he was face-to-face with her. She let go of his hand and cupped his face with her hand, kissing him very gently.

"I haven't been with anyone..." Conner whispered, just as she placed her index finger over his lips.

"Sssssshhhhhhhhhhhhhhh," Julia said. "I know." She planted another kiss on his flushed lips, this one even more passionate and firm.

"I don't know," Conner protested. "I just don't know," he repeated.

"Don't worry," Julia said. "I promise I'll take good care of you."

Julia grabbed both of Conner's hands and began to walk backward, glancing behind her to see the unmade bed in the bedroom. After they crossed the threshold, she swung him around and pushed him onto the bed.

CHAPTER 47

Bat, bat, bat. Conner slapped at the door of Joseph's studio, almost losing control of the coffee cup tray he was holding. He grabbed the tray by the side, securing the future of the two twin lattes he was bringing for him and his brother.

After a few minutes, Conner heard the door unlock and it swung toward him, nearly hitting the tray. Joseph emerged, squinting his eyes, clearly perplexed that Conner was even there.

Joseph pulled his respirator mask off of his nose and snapped it on the top of his head. "What are you doing here?"

"It's Thursday night. I brought the coffee," Conner said, as if his presence should have been expected.

Joseph pulled his head back, still squinting at his brother. "It's been months. I figured this was a broken tradition."

"Nah," Conner said casually. "Let's bring it back."

"Come in. Come in," Joseph said. "The door was locked because I wasn't expecting any company. Don't get me wrong, though, I'm so glad you're here."

Joseph swung the door wide open and motioned to Conner to come inside. With the other hand, he peeled the respirator mask off of his head and threw it down on the nearest table.

"So, what's up? How are things?" Joseph said excitedly, reaching for the cardboard cup that Conner presented him.

"Hit or miss," Conner said flatly. "I feel like the pain and loss is letting up and then it seems to come back with a vengeance, stronger than ever before."

"Sorry to hear that," Joseph said. "I can't imagine how hard this is on you. I just wish there was something I could do to take the pain away."

Joseph took a long slurp of his latte, looking back at the electric guitar project he had been working on. A classic Gibson Les Paul from the 1960s.

"What about you?" Conner inquired. "How's everything going?"

Joseph took a long sip of his coffee and pondered Conner's question for a moment.

"Not to piss on your parade, but things have been going really great," Joseph said, trying not to seem too excited. "I've never been busier here; it's like the word is out. I have all sorts of interesting, meaningful projects to work on, and I'm still able to go kayaking or hiking every weekend."

"That's great. I'm really pumped for you," Conner said, cracking an awkward smile.

"Yeah, it's cool," Joseph said. "Man, I'm just so glad you're here. Thank you for coming."

"Sure," Conner said with a clumsy expression, talking more casually than usual. "I did get lucky last night."

"What?" Joseph leapt off of his stool. "Are you kidding? Who? How?"

"Remember the Stradivarius?" Conner said as he searched for recognition in Joseph's face.

"The Stradivarius girl? You nailed the Stradivarius girl?" Joseph began to unconsciously hop up and down, excited like a dog involuntarily wagging its tail.

"Yeah," Conner said as his eyes dropped, clearly not sharing the excitement that his brother was expressing.

"Well, tell me all about it," Joseph pleaded. "What was it like?"

Conner answered his brother right off the bat. "Ah, it was actually, really... uh, awkward."

"Awkward," Joseph replied. "How so?"

"I don't know how to explain it," Conner said, searching for meaning. "I guess we just didn't fall into any rhythm. When we kissed, it was like she was moving up and down and I was moving side to side. We just weren't in sync. I couldn't even get it up at first, and then when I did, it... it just wasn't very good." Conner shook his head slowly and continued. "I mean, when Cassie and I were together, everything seemed to just fall into place. We were always in harmony. We moved in the same direction. It was almost like it was a symphony orchestra. With Julia, everything just felt wrong. It was just not a good fit. No chemistry."

Cutting his brother off, clearly seeing that he was becoming visibly upset by thinking of his connection with Cassie, Joseph said, "Have you ever thought that the kind of chemistry you had with Cassie took time to develop and didn't happen right away?"

Shaking his head harder this time, Conner puckered his lips. "Nah, it wasn't like that. I think we had immediate chemistry. I think you just have it, or you don't."

Joseph challenged his brother again. "Also, you aren't exactly in a good place to be intimate right now anyway. You're not over Cassie yet, and you're still in mourning."

"That's exactly what I told her," Conner yelled. "She just said that she'd take good care of my heart."

"Yikes," Joseph said. "She knows that Cassie passed, right?" Conner's head swung back toward Joseph. "Well, no, not exactly."

"Not exactly?" Joseph screamed incredulously. "What did you tell her?"

"Listen," Conner said firmly. "I told her I just got out of a relationship a few months ago. I didn't want to go into the whole Cassie thing. Every time I talk about it, I get deeply disturbed and I can't even finish sentences."

"I see," Joseph said as he was trying to calm himself down. "I totally get that, bro. Sorry for calling you out on it. I just think honesty is... you probably did the right thing."

A bit of steam escaped from the lid slit in Conner's coffee. He moved the cup to his lip and took a curdling sip.

"Well, anyway, I wouldn't put too much stock in your first time with a woman," Joseph advised. "Remember Jody? The yoga instructor?"

Conner moved his eyes from side to side and then nodded his head rapidly.

"The first time we were together was awful. I think we injured each other, and I split my lip open, which was funny in a way, but it resulted in us losing the mood entirely and we didn't even finish. But then we ended up building a very fulfilling physical, spiritual, and emotional relationship," Joseph said in a reassuring way. "I wouldn't count her out yet. Is she pretty?"

"She's, uh, definitely not my usual type, but I find her strangely attractive," Conner said confidently. "She's got red hair, big green eyes. Full pink lips. Really big ears and a wide nose, but they actually don't look out of place at all. It all works together really well."

"Well, there you go," Joseph said. "That's a great start. If she was a dog, I could see you not being able to connect with her physically."

Laughter emanated from Conner's lungs. He almost stopped himself because he was not used to laughing very much.

"Huhuh. Thanks, brother," Conner chortled. He then switched quickly to a flat affect. "I don't think I'm going to see her again, though."

"Are you out of your mind?" Joseph quizzically asked Conner. "You're telling me that you have a good-looking woman who is totally into you, she is a creative genius, and she's very caring, and you're going to stop seeing her? Now, Conner, I know the timing is not right, but I don't think you can let this one get away."

"Uh, yeah, I don't know," Conner said as he pondered the prospect of pursuing this relationship. "I hear what you're saying, but I'm just still experiencing so much emotional pain and depression over the loss of Cassie. I don't think this is the best move for me right now."

"OK," Joseph reasoned. "I get that this is not great timing, but when is timing great with life in general? I would argue very rarely. Maybe this is just the thing that can act as a distraction long enough to start healing the pain you're experiencing." Joseph took a big gulp of his latte and stared right into Conner's gray-blue eyes.

His eyes glancing down at the cardboard coffee cup, Conner assessed his brother's point of view. Yes, it wasn't the right time. Conner was clearly not over the death of his ex-fiancée. He wasn't over the loss that he felt every single day. The pain was not subsiding, but seemingly growing larger and more intense. However, Julia was a great person. Very intuitive, caring, nurturing. And she was also strong-willed. Not passive. She was confident, independent, determined, assertive. You don't often find all of those qualities in one woman.

"I don't know, maybe I'll see her again," Conner muttered. He and Joseph both took a deep swallow of coffee in unison.

CHAPTER 48

Tomorrow was the big day. Seth Warner would be with his sister, Sarah Warner, at her apartment in Bellevue. And that meant that tomorrow would be her last day on this earth.

He began to plan the operation in his mind, making sure to control for several contingencies. The delivery window was 5:00 p.m. to 7:00 p.m. He wanted to make sure to be there at 6:30 p.m. sharp to make absolutely, positively sure they would both be there.

He would go to the apartment and scope the floor out first to see if there were any open doors or people walking or milling around near the apartment. He would make sure he knew where the stairwell was, in case he had to make an exit that way. Conner also thought to himself that he would hit the elevator button to see how fast the elevator came to the eighth floor, which is where he assumed the apartment to be, given its number, 850.

To enter the apartment, Conner would first twist the doorknob to see if it was unlocked, which obviously would be ideal. If it wasn't, he would knock on the door and shout,

"Delivery," to see if that would entice someone to open the door.

If all else failed, Conner thought that he would attempt to kick in the door or maybe even shoot at the lock and handle to force it ajar, making sure to only use around four or five bullets, to ensure he saved at least ten for Sarah and a few extras just in case he needed them to finish Seth off if he attempted to attack Conner. He worked through counting out the bullets in his head, to make sure he didn't do what most people do in a dire situation, which is to empty the entire magazine.

After the killing, Conner thought that it would be best to back out of the door, still pointing the gun at Seth, and then hit the elevator's down button. If any other tenants emerged from their apartments, he would lunge the gun toward them and say, "Get back and shut the door."

If the cops happened to come quickly, he would drop the gun and cooperate, not wanting to cause a stir or chance getting shot by the police. Otherwise, he would walk briskly away, trying to find an opportunity to hail a taxi home.

"Am I really doing this?" Conner queried himself. "Is this for real?"

Not wanting a reason to talk himself out of it, he rose from his leather chair and paced around, grabbing the gun out of the junk drawer and gripping it with one and then both hands, chanting, "Cassie, Cassie, Cassie. I'm doing this for Cassie."

Conner conducted his routine. Pulling the magazine out of the gun, cocking the gun, dry firing the gun, pushing the magazine into the gun, pulling back the slide to make sure a bullet entered the chamber. Then pulling the magazine back out, pulling the slide to exit the bullet from the chamber, putting the bullet back in the magazine, and putting it back in the gun as a last step.

Conner returned to the junk drawer and placed the gun back gently and pushed the drawer closed with his forefinger.

He again began to chant to himself, "You are going to do this. This will take the pain away. This will transfer the pain to him. So you can feel happiness again."

CHAPTER 49

Conner woke up on his leather couch to a rapping at the door. He shook his head violently and began stumbling to the door. Conner lost his balance and righted himself right before he hit the door, placing his forearm on the door and resting his still-tired head on it as he leaned into the door.

"Who is it?" Conner coughed, clearing his throat and blinking his eyes rapidly.

"It's Julia, Conner. Can I come in?"

Conner whipped his head up and opened his eyes wide, shaking his head slowly back and forth. "Um, yeah, hang on a sec."

Conner fiddled with the lock and aggressively twisted it, pulling the door open to let her in.

"Thanks," Julia yelled as she darted into the apartment. She was wearing a head-to-toe raincoat, which she whipped off to reveal an emerald-green dress, which hugged her small frame. The green dress made her eyes illuminate, and they even seemed to sparkle. As Conner peered into her eyes, he was amazed at the dark green color, which was further accentuated by the green dress.

"How you feeling today?" Julia sang.

"I actually just woke up," Conner mumbled. "I feel exhausted."

"Well, let's go grab something to eat. Are you hungry?"

"Yeah, but it's pouring. How about sandwiches here?" Conner suggested.

Julia gave Conner a seductive look, and then turned and made her way to the refrigerator.

"Sounds like a good plan. Let's see what we've got here." Julia pulled out a bunch of vegetables and some Dijon mustard, throwing them on the counter. "Where are your utensils?" Julia innocently asked while reaching for the junk drawer.

Conner darted over and pinned himself between Julia and the drawer, not wanting her to discover his firearm. "Right over there." Conner pointed forcefully at the actual location of the flatware and clenched his teeth tightly.

"Oh, OK," Julia said casually, pulling the drawer open and fumbling with the butter knives, oblivious to the fact that Conner was deliberately blocking her from opening the junk drawer.

Julia made delectable sandwiches with honey-roasted ham, butter lettuce, mustard, shredded carrots, and sliced cucumbers. They enjoyed them at the table, staring out the window at the black and gray clouds, barely speaking.

"So, what do you have to drink?" Julia asked.

Conner looked at the refrigerator and answered, "I think we have orange juice, water, uh, club soda..."

"I'm talking about liquor, booze, alcohol," Julia interrupted.

"Oh, I believe I have some red wine in the pantry."

Julia gracefully rose and made her way to the pantry, looking at every shelf from top to bottom. "Oh, here it is." She grabbed the bottle from the neck and brought it close to her face.

"Chianti, love it. You know I went to school near Tuscany?"
Conner looked puzzled. "I did not know that."

"Yeah," she continued. It was actually the University of Siena, one of the most beautiful cities in Europe, in my opinion. I specifically went there because they have a very strong medical school." Julia began to open the bottle with the electronic bottle opener that was sitting on the counter.

Conner squinted, incredulous about her comment. "Do you even know how little sense that makes?"

"I know, right?" Julia giggled mischievously. "My dad's a surgeon, and he wanted me to be a doctor as well. But my great grandfather was a musician, and I found that I had much more talent, and interest, in music. So when he left me his violin in his will, I began to pursue music, and the rest is history."

"Interesting," Conner reflected. "Was your father upset with your decision?"

"He was," Julia said somberly. "He was... but when he saw how much my face lit up when I joined the symphony, and when he saw how talented I became, he became even more proud of me pursuing my passion than he ever was about my medical career."

Julia placed a glass in front of Conner, spilling red wine into a wine glass that looked more like a glass tulip.

"Thank you," Conner blurted out as he raised the glass to his lips and took a quick sip. "And thank you for the sandwich. It was quite good."

"Yeah, I'm not much of a cook, but I can make a mean sandwich."

Conner laughed a genuine laugh. "Well, again, thank you. This is much better than running out to get something to eat."

Conner glanced out the window and back at Julia as they enjoyed their wine, killing the entire bottle in about thirty minutes. They talked about their childhoods. Conner's career path. His love for teaching and for mentoring kids. Julia talked about her time in Italy and other adventures traveling throughout Europe. Conner nearly forgot about the pain of his loss for a split second, but as he closed his eyes and tried to forget, the pain came back even worse than ever before. It wasn't going away. It was getting worse.

CHAPTER 50

Julia approached Conner, put her hand gently on his head, and jerked his hand away from his empty glass.

"Now I know we got off to a pretty rough start, but let's try again."

Conner pulled his arms away instinctively. He began to say something and then just shut his mouth tight. He looked at Julia with understanding, rose from the chair, and followed her to the couch. They both fell on their sides, heads hitting the cushion. He began to get very flustered and anxious, not wanting to repeat what happened last time, but he was mesmerized by her stunning green eyes. Although they were not as complex and dimensional as Cassie's, they were a unique color of green. He was enthralled by them.

"All right, let's take this slow," Julia whispered. "Take off my dress."

Conner slowly moved his arms around her body, found the zipper after a moment, and pulled it down very slowly. He then pinched the fabric around her shoulders and shook the straps around her arms and pulled the dress down her body, all the while watching her slender body squirm around to enable the dress to slide off of her.

She was wearing orange panties and a matching bra, which had an uncanny resemblance to her fiery red hair.

"Now your turn," Conner said as he pulled her hand to his shirt, not wanting simply to be a passive participant in this act.

Julia grabbed his shirt and pulled it above his head and threw it all the way over to the other side of the room. She then gently unbuckled his pants, unbuttoned and unzipped his jeans, and pushed them down to his knees, where he took over and shook them off by rolling his ankles and feet back and forth until they came off.

Julia hopped on top of him and began kissing him. This time, they weren't out of sync at all. As her lips pressed up against his, he felt flushed with passion and emotion. He began feeling an overwhelming sense of calm, and a buzzed feeling.

Julia reached back to unclasp her bra, revealing her teardrop breasts. Conner cupped them gently and reached up to kiss her again, feeling more and more at peace. At this point, Conner felt high, as though a heavy dose of opium started being slowly introduced into his bloodstream. He imagined this feeling to be close to what the first dose of heroin feels like, the one that addicts chase after for the rest of their lives but never achieve. His entire body felt good. Every sense was heightened. He felt peaceful, warm, calm, and sensitive. He did not want this feeling to stop.

Conner nudged Julia and she fell onto her back. They stripped what was left of each other's clothes off and started making love. All the while, Conner felt this amazing sensation, the heroin feeling, as he referred to it. He wasn't sure why he felt this way. He wasn't sure what exactly caused it.

But he knew that it was different. He'd never felt this way while making love to anyone.

They both reached orgasm simultaneously and slammed down on the couch, both breathing heavily. Julia was flushed, her normally pale face now red, almost as if she was blushing for an extended period of time. Conner kept shaking his head with disbelief. He was still feeling, and enjoying, the extremely pleasurable feeling that began when he started kissing her. He didn't want that feeling to subside, but he knew it would, and the painful memories and overwhelming sense of loss would return. Conner didn't want those feelings to come, so he dwelled on the opiate-like sensation that he'd felt and was still feeling. He was hooked.

Conner and Julia both dozed off into very deep and restful sleeps. Conner began to uncharacteristically snore, which jerked Julia awake for a moment, but she just smiled and fell back to sleep, putting her hand over his and grasping it tightly.

CHAPTER 51

Conner got up the next day, blinking his eyes rapidly until he could make out the large red numbers on the alarm clock: 12:47 p.m.

"Holy fuck," Conner exclaimed. "How did I sleep so late?"

Julia was nowhere to be found, but he noticed some words scrawled on the back of a receipt on his nightstand.

"Good afternoon, sleepy head. I have to run some errands. Dinner tomorrow? Love, Julia."

"Oh God." Conner crumpled up the receipt and threw it toward the kitchen.

Conner sat up in his bed and began to look angry. He wanted to focus his every effort at the task at hand.

"No distractions. Tonight's the night. Eyes on the prize."

Conner began to throw the covers off of himself and stammer toward the bathroom. Twisting the knob in his shower, he turned it up higher than normal, wanting to take a scorching-hot shower to purify himself physically, emotionally, and spiritually before his covert mission later in the night.

As Conner put his face under the scalding water, he began to reflect on the loss of his dear Cassie. How she died so viciously. How she probably screamed for help and mercy. How he was going to avenge her death in a most appropriate way.

Visualizing flashbacks of this pain gave him the power and bravery to go through with this. He knew that he would feel lifelong pain and loss because of this callous act, and the only way to truly make Seth pay for this would be to make him feel this same excruciating pain and loss.

After the shower, Conner got ready in a very slow and robotic fashion. He shaved in the sink, which was very uncharacteristic for him, as he usually did it in the shower to save time. He chose to dress in all black to blend in with the night as much as he could.

Conner kept grabbing the gun out of the drawer. He'd put it in his pocket, pull it out, place it in his waistline along the small of his back, pull it out, point it at the wall, and squeeze the trigger, repeating his ritual. He decided that because it was so big and bulky that it would be best to carry it in his waistline, because that would make it easily accessible as well.

Once he was ready, he heard a strong noise emanating from his stomach. It was growling. He stared at the clock and noticed that it was 2:17 p.m. He hadn't eaten since almost twenty-four hours before.

Conner ran toward his phone, tapping on his brother's name to call him, figuring that this may be his last meal as a free man, so he might as well spend it with someone he cared about deeply.

"Hey, Conner," Joseph said with a giddy ring to his voice.

"Hi, brother, want to grab something to eat?" Conner was also verbally excited.

"Oh, I just ate," Joseph said disappointedly. "I'll go with you and watch you eat, though." He wasn't about to lose out on the opportunity to hang out with his brother.

"Cool, man, can you meet me at the People's Burger food truck in thirty?"

Joseph rubbed his chin as if he was making an already made decision. "I'll be there, bud."

CHAPTER 52

When Conner arrived, Joseph was already there, perusing the menu to see if he could grab something small so he wouldn't have to make his brother eat alone.

They both approached the counter at the same time. It was well after lunch hour so there was no one else in line.

"I'll have the homemade tots," Joseph yelled.

"You don't have to get anything. You already ate. Oh, I'll have a jalapeño burger and, uh, some French fries."

"Anything to drink?" said the lady in the food truck.

"Two bottles of water," Conner shouted as he flashed two fingers in the air. A second later he received two frosty bottles of Fiji water.

"So, what's up?" Joseph inquired.

Conner looked at him, bewildered. "Does something have to be up? Just wanted to hang out one... one fine Saturday afternoon."

"Nope. Absolutely not," Joseph replied. "Just curious. So, how's Stradivarius girl?"

Again, Conner shot Joseph another confused look. "Is that all you care about?"

Joseph bobbed his head up and down excitedly. "Yup, pretty much."

"OK, first of all, she's not Stradivarius girl, her name is Julia. Jesus. You make her out to be some sort of horsehair-slinging superhero or something."

"Oh em gee," Joseph expressed quizzically. "You totally dig this chick. I can't believe it."

"Are you out of your ever-loving mind?" Conner shrieked. "I'm still in mourning. I can't even begin to think about other women."

"OK, tell me you haven't been with her over the past few days. Just tell me that, and I'll leave you alone." Joseph looked deeply into Conner's face to identify any chinks in his armor.

"All right, we were together last night," Conner relented.

"Together, together together? Like bumpin' uglies together?" Joseph giggled a little bit.

"You are so vulgar," Conner stated firmly with a sour face. "But, yes, we actually did."

"So, was she a dead fish this time?" Joseph asked.

"She's not a dead fish. But, for your information, it was actually good this time. Not like the deep connection I had with Cassie, but it felt unbelievably good physically. It was definitely different. But definitely good."

"I'm so happy to hear that," Joseph said as he applauded lightly. "So are you going to see her again?"

"Order's up," a female voice emanated from the food truck.

Conner ran over and grabbed their food. They plopped down across from each other at a nearby table.

"I don't know if I'm going to see her or not. She wants to have dinner tomorrow, but..." Conner drifted off into a long pause.

Joseph slowed his roll. "Do you want to see her again?"

Conner took a slow breath. "She seems great, but I have so many emotions that I'm dealing with—mostly pain, depression, and loss. I don't know if I want to bring someone into that world. It's really pretty dark right now." Conner squeezed his sandwich and took a gigantic bite as grease ran down his fingers.

"I get that," Joseph said in a calm manner. "I just think that timing is everything in life. And sometimes the timing's not right. But what if you don't find another girl like this for a long time. She seems really nice, smart, caring, passionate. And it doesn't hurt that she's not a dead fish."

Conner shook his head swiftly. "You're such a perv," he said through a mouthful of burger.

"Hahahahahahahaha," Joseph laughed uncontrollably. "I had to. I couldn't help myself. God, the look on your face. Classic."

"I'll think about it," Conner said as he wiped his hands off with a brown napkin. "I'll think about it."

Joseph dunked a few tots in some ketchup and tossed them into his mouth. They continued to speak about Conner's mental state. About Joseph's booming business. About what the future held. All Conner could think about was that someone was going to die tonight.

CHAPTER 53

Conner returned home without Joseph and grabbed the Glock 19. He decided to take an Uber and get dropped off several blocks from Seth's sister's apartment.

After locking the door on his apartment, he headed toward the harbor. He wanted to look at the beautiful water one last time before he headed off for his mission. He remembered many times how he walked or stood at the waterfront with Cassie. Holding her hand. Gazing into her hazel eyes. Feeling so much attraction and love. He wanted to experience those feelings again.

This motherfucker has to pay, Conner thought to himself. He began to get really angry and remember the unbearable pain he had felt—and that he would continue to feel for his entire life.

Conner reached back and touched the gun that was nestled against his lower back. It felt cold to the touch but warm against his back because it had absorbed his body heat.

He began to weep as he watched the water move and ripple. He couldn't believe his life took such a turn. What was once full of promise had turned into misery and disgust. He couldn't believe someone could take such an innocent life. He imagined Seth overpowering her, slicing her up multiple times, seeing the blood splatter all over the floor, and not feeling anything for her. Conner began to rub his eyes and wipe the tears away with both palms of his hands.

As his mind wandered, Conner thought about what his brother said. Sure, the timing wasn't right to be with another woman, but would the time ever be right? Could this be a sign from above? God telling him that he needed someone in his life to help him through this painful and difficult time? If he shared the reason he was so "hollow," could she help him heal in a more intentional way?

Conner shook his head, wiped additional tears that had accumulated on his cheeks, and touched the gun again to make sure it was there. His Uber appeared in front of him.

"Let's do this," Conner said as he rose from his seated position. "There it is," Conner said in a booming voice as he stared at the Uber, a silver Toyota Camry.

The late-model Camry slowed down, brakes squealing as if they hadn't been serviced for forty thousand miles.

Conner hopped in the vehicle and put his head down so he couldn't be recognized.

"Overlake Hospital," Conner said, reinforcing the location he tapped into the app. He selected that location because it was close to Sarah's apartment.

The Uber driver stepped on the gas.

CHAPTER 54

Eeeeeeeeeeeeeeeeeeeeeeer. The Camry came to a stop in front of the emergency room entrance of Overlake Hospital with heavily squeaking brakes.

Conner zipped out of the cab and started walking west.

Conner kept his head down, looking at his black sweatshirt. The weather was very cool, but it wasn't raining. There were scattered clouds but not a drop of rain.

Conner walked rapidly down 12th Street, and he kept grabbing at the gun to make sure he didn't unintentionally leave it anywhere, like in the Uber. He glanced to his right and saw something out of his peripheral vision, and he stopped dead in his tracks.

It was a flower stand. What a perfect way to get into the apartment. If he held the flowers up against the peephole, he would be able to avoid detection. Surely Seth knew who Conner was because he saw him as he stalked his victim, and he would know better than to open the door.

"I'll have this one, please," Conner said gently as he picked up a rather bountiful bouquet of peonies.

"That will be twenty-three dollars," the florist said.

Conner pulled some cash out of his wallet and handed it to her. "Keep the change," he said as he darted back in his original direction.

Conner slowed down deliberately. He felt that he was walking too fast and almost jumping out of his skin with purpose and excitement. He decided to walk more slowly because he wanted to control his actions. He wanted to be very methodical about what he was doing and not get too emotional or erratic. He was there to kill Seth's sister. That's it. He was afraid if he succumbed to his emotions or lost control, that would be enough for Seth to seize his gun and use it against himself. Conner was not going to let that happen.

Conner made sure to not attract too much attention, so he kept the flower arrangement pointed down toward the ground and didn't swing it back and forth as he swung his arms.

Conner arrived at the apartment building and walked over to the wall. He placed his back against the wall and put the back of his head on the wall, looking up at the black sky. His gun clinked against the wall, so he was positive it was still there.

He started to get a funny feeling. I was like nothing he had ever felt before. It wasn't fear or excitement or nervousness. It might have been a little of all three. His stomach started feeling funny and tingling, like a pleasant form of nausea. The skin all over his body started to become numb and feel very warm, the exact opposite of the weather. He felt disoriented and lightheaded. His mouth began to get dry. Conner started to take deep breaths and repeat the following phrase: "I'm going to do this. I'm going to do this. I'm *going* to do this."

Conner walked slowly and steadily to the front door, swinging it open with his hand. He felt a vibration in his pocket. He fetched his phone and saw he had a missed call from an unknown number. He thought nothing of it as he headed for the elevator and punched the button. A few seconds later, the light above the elevator illuminated and he heard a loud *ding*.

No one departed from the elevator. It was completely empty. Conner handed the bouquet of flowers from his left hand to his right hand and extended his pointed finger to the array of buttons and stabbed the one labeled "8."

The doors closed. The elevator moved. Conner took one last long deep breath and exhaled slowly.

Ding.

CHAPTER 55

The doors opened and an older gentleman with long gray hair stood there. Conner twisted his body to the right and moved out of the elevator. The old man nodded once at him and entered the elevator. After the doors closed, Conner moved around the floor, looking for other people that he may have to deal with or avoid. He noticed that apartment 850 was down the hall to the right, so he made his way over there. He began to get the funny feeling again, so he kept on taking deep breaths to make it subside.

Conner arrived at apartment number 850. He pressed his ear up against the door and heard voices, so he knew they were in there. He lifted the gun up out of his waistline and dropped the flowers on the ground. Conner clicked the safety off and visually inspected it to make sure it was off. He pressed the button on the side of the gun near the trigger to release the magazine. He noticed that there were live bullets in the top of the magazine, and he turned the magazine to the side to see that there were fifteen bullets, and another fifteen in his other magazine.

Conner slid the magazine back in slowly and made sure it clicked into place. He pulled the slide back forcefully and quickly, watching it insert one of the fifteen nine-millimeter bullets into the chamber. The gun was now loaded and cocked. All he had to do now was pull the trigger. He bent back down and grabbed the bouquet with his left hand.

He looked down the hallway on both sides and saw no one. He wiped some clammy sweat that accumulated on his forehead and approached the door, knocking five times loudly.

"Delivery," Conner said in a low, gravelly voice.

It seemed like a hundred years before he heard anything. He pushed the bouquet up against his nose to cover the bottom half of his face and show whoever was looking through the peephole that it was indeed flowers that were being delivered.

Sheesh. Clock. The door unlocked. The door opened slowly, only about eight or nine inches. Seth's head appeared quickly with a deadpan face. Conner flinched instinctively, still obscuring half of his face with the flowers. Noticing that there was no chain on the door, he did exactly what he planned to do. He lowered his head even farther, put his shoulder down, and ran forcefully into the door as fast as he possibly could.

CHAPTER 56

The door swung open and Seth fell back seven feet. He touched the floor with his hand and regained his balance right as Conner grabbed the door and closed it slowly and quietly, stepping over the flowers that had fallen on the ground a few seconds earlier.

Click, the door exclaimed. Conner pointed the gun at Seth's head with both hands and looked at him with irate eyes.

Seth was taller than Conner had imagined. Six feet five maybe. Seth had a somber look on his face. He bowed his head with a look of fear, and he began breathing rapidly. There were loud noises coming from the kitchen. The sink was on. Some sort of mixer or blender was running.

Conner noticed that his palms were sweating clammy sweat and lubricating the trigger. He didn't want to take any chances, so he switched hands, wiping his right hand on the side of his jeans and on his black sweatshirt. He exchanged the guns between his hands again, lunging the gun toward Seth to communicate that he had him covered. He aimed right at his skull, and there was no way to lunge at Conner or escape.

Conner took one eye off of Seth for a split second, looking toward the kitchen. He surveyed the rest of the apartment, making sure there were no other threats. He looked back at Seth and shot daggers from his milky blue eyes to Seth's face.

"You know me," Conner said in a soft, calm voice without phrasing the statement as a question. "Don't you?"

Seth shrugged, beginning to show more emotion and fear. His breathing became even more and more rapid.

"But you don't know why I'm here," Conner quipped. "Sarah," Conner yelled out, not concerned about the volume of his voice this time.

Conner stepped back even farther, touching his back against the wall at one end of the apartment. He wanted to make sure to put ample space between Seth and him. Conner wanted to be as careful and cautious as possible.

A slender woman appeared from beyond the wall where the kitchen was, grabbing the wall with her left hand.

"What the hell is going..." The woman stoically asked this question and then stopped dead in her tracks. She looked at Conner with shock and panic, and then looked back at her brother, who was breathing hard and obviously fearful.

The woman wasn't Sarah Warner. It was Julia.

CHAPTER 57

Conner stepped back again, hitting the wall hard, blinking, and then pushing the gun farther toward Seth. "Don't you fucking move, asshole. I got you." Conner continued to deliberately speak at a low volume.

He averted his eyes to Julia again, incredulous.

"What the fuck are you doing here?" Conner gurgled as he looked back at Seth, making sure to grip the gun tighter as he noticed both hands shaking uncontrollably.

"I *am* Sarah," Julia screamed, tears beginning to well up in her emerald-green eyes.

"That's impossible. Your name is Julia Farelli. You're not Sarah Warner." Conner's voice began to crack. "Stay the fuck back or you're dead, Seth."

Seth stepped back, not wanting to put his sister in harm's way. He again looked at Conner with a combination of hatred and anger. His squarish glasses moved up slightly as he squinted his eyes, looking for an opening to bum-rush Conner.

"I go by my middle name. I've always gone by my middle name. I kept my married name because of my career. Conner, please put down the gun," Julia pleaded.

"Conner? How do you know him?" Seth stared angrily at Julia with a deadpan expression.

"Don't answer that," Conner commanded. "Don't say a fucking word, Seth. I will pull this trigger and end your life right now." Conner's voice began to rise.

Conner pressed the side of the gun against his forehead and pointed it right back at Seth. He started to get nervous. The funny feeling was washed away by fear and disgust, shock and pain.

"You are *not* Sarah. I saw Sarah at the restaurant. The night we met. She was having dinner with Seth. She was brunette. She was wearing... She was wearing..." Conner trailed off.

Julia's eyes began to leak as she blinked. "It wasn't me," Julia begged. "It wasn't me. I was out on the street with you. Remember?"

"Oh God, how the fuck did this happen?" Conner began to pace back and forth, keeping the gun trained on Seth with every step.

"Do you know what this scumbag did?" Conner continued to pace and mutter to himself.

Julia began to cry, pulling her fists up to her eyes to wipe the tears away. She shook her head rapidly and looked back at Conner.

"He killed my fiancée. That's right. He almost killed her when they were in college, and he came and finished the job a few months ago." Conner stopped dead in his tracks and pointed the gun at Seth with both hands.

Julia looked over at her brother, waiting for a reaction. Waiting for a denial. Waiting for anything. All she saw was a mixture of anger and mania, a frustrated smirk punctuated by a grimace.

"Do you know why I'm here?" Conner went back to his low, guttural tone of voice, and he pointed this question at Seth. "Do you know why I'm here?"

"I can only imagine you've come to kill me," Seth muttered.

"Nope. That's not it." Conner clenched his teeth and swung the gun toward Julia. "I'm here to kill her."

CHAPTER 58

"What are you talking about? What are you doing?" Julia sniffled. "Kill me?"

"That's the only way," Conner said in a somber voice. "That's the only way I'll be free of this."

"What the hell are you talking about, Conner? Do you understand what you're saying? Why are you doing this?"

Conner pointed the gun back at Julia, who stepped back toward the kitchen. He directed the gun back at Seth after a brief moment. Conner's legs were now shaking. He regained control of his hands, but he was still sweating profusely. His palms were sweating, his forehead was sweating, and his feet were sweating.

"Listen," Seth piped up. "I do know Cassie. We dated. We went through a bad breakup. After college I sought out therapy, and I've been in counseling for more than a decade. I promise you I haven't seen Cassie in more than a decade."

Conner thought to himself about his situation. What was the right move? He had been focused on one thing and one thing only for months: killing Seth's sister, whoever she was. That was the only way to make Seth feel the agonizing and extended pain that Conner had felt and would feel for the rest of his life.

What now, though? Was Joseph right? Was Julia his only hope for stitching his heart back together and finding someone other than Cassie to be with forever? Would killing her cause even more pain? Was Conner truly prepared to spend the rest of his life in jail for this? Was he falling in love with Julia?

"Fuck," Conner yelled at the top of his lungs, pointing the gun back and forth between Seth and Julia, who Conner now knew was actually Sarah.

And why not just kill Seth? This would likely satisfy his appetite for revenge and was his original intention in the first place. But what if Seth was honest and he wasn't the killer? And if he went through with it, would Julia report him to the police and hate him for the rest of her life?

Should he spare both of them and run out of the apartment?Kill himself? Surely that would alleviate the pain he'd dragged with him over the last several months.

"Conner," Julia urged. "Please, please, please, put the gun down. Let's talk about this. You know I'm here for you. I care about you. You know that."

Seth looked back at Julia and back at Conner. His face quickly went from fear to frustration.

"There's only one way to take the pain away," Conner whispered.

Conner pointed the gun at Julia and squeezed the trigger, but it didn't go off because he didn't pull it down all the way.

He swiftly moved the barrel of the gun to Seth's chest. He let his finger off the trigger and then pulled on it again. Again, the gun didn't go off because he released his finger from the trigger at the last moment. He dropped to his knees with the gun still aimed at Seth's body.

"Why, God?" Conner cried as tears ran down his face. "Why this?"

Conner touched the top of the gun against his forehead and began to cry and rock back and forth. Seth began to slowly move toward Conner.

Conner took the gun away from his forehead, pressed the barrel against his temple, looked into Julia's incredibly beautiful green eyes, and fingered the trigger again.

Just then, Conner's phone began to vibrate forcefully. He dropped to a sitting position and placed the top of the gun against his forehead.

Conner fished his phone out of his pocket and looked at the caller, while dragging the gun across his face to scrape his tears away. It was Detective Stevens. He quickly pressed it to his ear, keeping the gun in his other hand propped against his forehead.

"Hello," Conner inquired sheepishly. "Hi, Detective Stevens. What's up?"

"Conner, I just wanted to update you on the case with Cassie. We have a suspect in custody. His name is Daniel Knox. Do you know such a person?"

Conner's ears perked up, rapidly searching his memory while scanning the room, which started to spin. "I don't know who that is. I can't recall anyone by that name."

"Apparently he worked with her. We found a possible murder weapon, a box cutter that we found in his garage," Stevens conveyed.

"Oh my God," Conner said. Dan from her work. The one who had a crush on her. It wasn't Seth after all.

Conner dropped the phone on the floor. He pulled the gun away from his head and dropped it away from his body. He put his hands on his temples and moaned loudly.

"I can't believe this," Conner yelled. "This can't be happening. This is unbelievable."

Conner looked over Julia's eyes and Seth's eyes, not knowing what to think. All his planning and investments had been for nothing. He slowly picked himself up from the apartment floor, collected his possessions, and stumbled out of the apartment, knowing full well that Seth was not the murderer. And not knowing where to go from here.

- THE END -

Made in the USA
Monee, IL
06 February 2022

90604084R00105